the Alliance

Becoming Beka Book 2

the Alliance

Sarah
Anne
Sumpolec

MOODY PUBLISHERS
CHICAGO

All Scripture quotations are taken from the *Holy Bible, New International Version*®. NIV®. Copyright © 1973, 1978, 1984 by International Bible Society. Used by permission of Zondervan Publishing House. All rights reserved.

Cover Images: © 2004 Grace\Masterefile

Library of Congress Cataloging-in-Publication Data

Sumpolec, Sarah Anne.
    The alliance / Sarah Anne Sumpolec.
        p. cm.—(Becoming Beka series)
    Summary: Beka returns to school with a newfound faith, which is put to the test when play rehearsals bring her close to Gretchen, who is becoming involved in the occult and launches a smear campaign against Beka's Christian friend, Lori.
    ISBN 0-8024-6452-1
    [1. Theater—Fiction. 2. Occultism—Fiction. 3. High schools—Fiction. 4. Schools—Fiction. 5. Christian life—Fiction.] I. Title.

PZ7.S9563Al 2004
[Fic]—dc22

                                                    2003025062

1 3 5 7 9 10 8 6 4 2

Printed in the United States of America

To my Molly Rose
Your joyous arrival will forever be entwined
with the writing of this book. You are an angel.

ACKNOWLEDGMENTS

While writing is a rather solitary affair, the birth of a book takes so many. I'd like to thank the team at Moody, especially Michele Straubel, who believed in this project, Cheryl Dunlop for her editing prowess, and Barbara LeVan Fisher for her wonderful cover designs. A heartfelt thanks also goes to Dave Talbot and the Mount Hermon faculty, whose wonderful conference paved the way for this series, and to Janet Kobobel Grant, who provides such gracious support and guidance.

Thank you also to my writing friends who read, critiqued, and were excited for me throughout this whole process. A special thank-you to Mary Custalow for being such a wonderful cheerleader and friend. And to my many online friends who answered questions and rejoiced with me through the small accomplishments, especially Wendy Lawton, who introduced me to all the right people, I am in your debt.

I can't leave out my wonderful husband, Jeff, who encouraged me even when I was tired and cranky from round-the-clock feedings, and my two little princesses, Lydia and Cassie Joy, who were understanding and patient even when Mommy had to work at the computer so much. (Mama, you've been working forever!)

And always, a very special thank-you to Jesus Christ —without Him there would be no book and no me. To Him be the all the glory and praise.

My whole new chance at life was not turning out as I had hoped. It's kind of easy to think that you'll be able to reinvent yourself, to change the course of your life with a single decision. But then you turn around and you are facing the same people, who look at you in the same way they always have.

I knew I wanted things to be different. Even sort of believed they could be different. But something happened as I walked down the hall that first morning after the New Year. The first time I walked down the hallway of the school I had attended for the past two and a half years. My first time as a new believer. What happened was . . . nothing. Absolutely nothing. I still felt very much like the same Rebekah Madison of two weeks ago. And I began to wonder if anything was really going to change at all.

*　　*　　*

"Hey, Madison!" I turned to the sound of Gretchen Stanley's voice commanding my attention. She always commanded attention from anyone nearby. I was glad we were on amiable terms, but when Gretchen called, you had to jump. I wasn't sure I wanted to jump for anybody.

But today, I jumped.

"Yeah, what's up?" I smiled.

Liz, Mai, and Theresa hovered nearby. They looked so much like Charlie's Angels standing there waiting for their orders that I almost laughed. Theresa was a tall red-head, Mai was a younger, meaner version of Lucy Liu, only with shorter hair, and Liz was totally Cameron Diaz, complete with long smooth blonde hair and a certain "airhead" quality. I noticed immediately that Chrissy wasn't nearby, and I realized I hadn't seen her with the group recently. They seemed to mostly travel as a unit. Chrissy must have been blacklisted for some reason and Liz, who usually hovered near the outskirts, and who was trying hard to shed her Lizzy nickname, had moved into the "inner circle." It was all kind of ridiculous, but I knew my life at school was much better since I was no longer in "social Siberia." For a moment I felt sorry for Chrissy, and I didn't even know her.

Gretchen turned to them and shooed them away, rolling her eyes as she did so. Once they moved away she gave her blonde curls an extra toss—surely meant for someone other than me—as she pulled me close.

"Have I got a secret for you! You won't believe what I found out over winter break."

"What?" I asked, genuinely curious, not only about the secret but her desire to pull me back into "the know."

"Not heeeere," she said dramatically. "We'll talk before rehearsal. You just stick close to me, Madison, and I'll watch your back." She turned and shimmied down the hallway, waving and giggling at her public. I watched her go, wondering for the millionth time why she was so popular. She was cute and built well, but there was nothing extraordinary about her. And even though her skin seemed tan and flawless, she also had this narrow nose that turned up a bit at the end, which made her look even more stuck up. I turned back to my locker. Even though it was pointless to worry about what Gretchen's big secret was, I did. All day.

*   *   *

"Well, you'll just have to wait and see what she tells you. Don't stress about it." Lori was overly calm about my news at the lunch table.

"But what if it's . . . you know. About what happened over break."

Lori's eyes grew large, apparently just cluing in to the depth of my anxiety. "But how would she know about that? Who knows about it?"

"Just my family. And you."

"Then she can't know. They have confidentiality

things at those places. Don't worry. I'm sure it's some dumb rumor about some guy she likes."

"I hope you're right."

"I am. Now on to more interesting topics. Have you seen Mark today?"

I grinned in spite of myself. "A couple of times. You know, we've only been back a couple of hours, and he's all I can think about. Well, him and Gretchen's big secret. That can't be good."

"But at least it's normal."

"Yeah, but we talked about this. I prayed with you that night to put Mark into God's hands and let Him lead me. But my heart seems to have a mind of its own."

Lori thought for a moment before she answered. "Look, all I know is that we're brand-new at this whole Jesus thing. He must understand. We'll just keep trying." She took a deep breath. "Yep, we'll just keep trying."

"We? I thought I was the one with all the heart problems. 'Fess up. What aren't you telling me?"

Lori dropped her head, letting her long dark waves fall across her face. "I've been spending an inordinate amount of time thinking about Mark's friend Brian."

"What? You didn't tell me that! I thought we were friends." I pouted.

"Oh, we are!" She looked up quickly. "Forever friends. I guess I have been trying denial. It isn't working."

"Well, aren't we a pair?" I said, gathering up my lunch things.

"Yeah. You've got that right."

*　　*　　*

I was so glad that Lori had moved to town. Even though we had been friends only a few short weeks, I felt closer to her than I had ever felt to anybody. I don't suppose many friends can say that they both made a life-changing decision on the same day. We had been over at Lori's house, and her foster mother, Megan, had shared with us about Jesus in a way I had never really understood before. That day, both Lori and I had made commitments to follow Christ. We were in it together, and it helped to know I had someone rooting for me.

That's why I felt a pang of guilt as I walked to my next class. The one thing Lori didn't know was how much Gretchen hated her. Lori wasn't stupid. She knew full well that Gretchen wasn't interested in being friends with her, and it didn't bother her. But I couldn't bring myself to tell Lori about Gretchen's true feelings. Gretchen was just jealous, but she was also lethal. She had single-handedly made my life at school a nightmare after my mother's death. She had an ability to sway public opinion any way she wanted, and right now she wanted Lori alienated.

In truth, I still hadn't figured out why Gretchen had changed her mind about me in the first place. She had all of a sudden gone from publicly persecuting me to inviting me back to the "in crowd." I liked being popular again, but how long I could stay there I wasn't sure.

*　　*　　*

Gretchen had convinced me to try out for the school's musical, *Annie,* before Christmas last year. I had earned the part of Molly—one of the orphans who is friends with Annie—and Gretchen had gotten the title role. I was surprised she could fit her head through the auditorium door.

"Beka! There you are." She grabbed my arm and pulled me through the side door of the stage into a hallway.

"Gretchen. Rehearsal is going to start in like three minutes. We'd better go back in."

"Oh, please. They can't start without me. I'm Annie. Remember?"

As if I could forget, I thought.

"I have to tell you what I found out this weekend!" I took a deep breath, bracing myself. If she had found out about my hospitalization, my life as I knew it would be over.

"Well, I just happened to overhear my mother talking to my dad about this 'sweet little case' she had been assigned. You know she's a court-appointed advocate, right?"

I nodded, still not sure where the conversation was headed.

"Well, I could only hear bits and pieces of the conversation, but I figured out that the case involved a sixteen-year-old girl being adopted. Apparently it's a pretty unusual case. Well, of course, I just had to find out the rest of the story. I mean, people depend on me for accurate information."

She paused, looking at me to agree with her. I nodded but felt sick to my stomach. Now I knew exactly where the conversation was headed.

"After my mom went to bed I took a look through her briefcase. I figured whoever it was must go to our school since it's a Bragg County case. Of course, I didn't find any actual papers, but I found a note in her planner about a meeting with . . . are you ready? Trent! Rollins and Trent. It's Lori! That obnoxious new girl is an orphan!" She waited for a moment and then pushed my shoulder. "What's wrong with you? Isn't that the most interesting bit of gossip we've ever had in this dull school?"

"Gretchen, you can't tell anybody that."

"Who, me? Beka, I have a responsibility to protect the people of this school."

"Protect them from what? So she's an orphan. For the moment anyway. What's the big deal?"

"How did she become an orphan? Huh? What if she murdered her parents or . . ."

"You can't be serious."

"I warned you that there was something wrong with that girl—I just know there's some sordid story in this somewhere. I'm your friend, Beka. I know that you're trying to be nice to her and all, but you're being terribly naive. I'm trying to help you."

"There's no story, and you can't just go around telling people about it. It should be her decision." I said the words firmly, but I was shaking inside.

"You knew about it, didn't you? Didn't you? How did her parents die?"

"That's none of our business." I decided to switch to a different tactic. "Look, Gretchen, I'm asking you, as your friend, not to say anything about this. Please."

She looked at me carefully as she pulled at a blonde curl.

"Sure, Beka. I won't say anything." She paused and leaned in closer. "But you owe me," she added.

"Owe you?"

"Yeah, I'll keep your little friend's secret—for now. But you owe me."

Suddenly the door flew open next to us and slammed against the cement wall, causing us both to jump. It was Mai, her silky black hair flying as she stopped short.

"You two better get in here. T is ticked."

We followed Mai back into the auditorium and slipped into some seats, but our entrance did not go unnoticed.

"That is the one and only time you will be late for one of my rehearsals," Mr. Thompson, the director, called from the stage. "Do it again and I will replace you, got it?"

We both nodded, but Gretchen didn't seem to care.

*   *   *

By the time I reached home I could feel my shoulders knotting up from the tension. T, which is what most kids called Mr. Thompson, was not a very laid-back type of guy—just the opposite in fact. The rehearsal schedule he had handed out looked like it came from a man who was oblivious to the fact that we all had to go to school while we prepared for the play. He scared me. Gretchen seemed to think he was harmless, but I had never been around anybody who was so completely . . . intense.

"So how was the first rehearsal?" Paul asked as soon as I came into the kitchen.

"Not bad." I shrugged. "Has Thompson always been so . . ."

Paul grinned. "You get used to it."

"You quit the band, remember?"

"Yeah, but not because of Thompson. He just takes everything dead seriously. It's not just a school musical to him. In his mind you all are opening on Broadway."

I leaned on the counter where Paul was slicing cucumbers for dinner. "Do you think it's . . . I don't know . . . weird? That I'm in the play?"

He stopped slicing and looked over at me. "No. Not at all. It's not something I had ever imagined you being interested in, but I think it'll be good for you. See how it turns out when it's all over."

"Yeah, you're right. Do you need any help with dinner?"

"Nah, I've got it. Hopefully Mary will be back soon. I'm getting kind of bored with spaghetti." He grinned.

"Me too," I admitted. "Well, I guess I'll try to get some homework done before dinner."

He nodded his head and gave me a sympathetic smile before I left. Paul had offered to cover dinners while our housekeeper, Mary, was training somebody to care for her elderly mother. Mary had been helping out with the housework and dinner ever since my mother died, but while she cooked all sorts of wonderful things, Paul had been alternating between spaghetti, hot dogs, and frozen lasagna.

I smiled as I went up the stairs. I was so glad that Paul

and I weren't fighting anymore. It felt nice to be able to finally take a deep breath and relax while I was at home.

*   *   *

I really did try to get started on my English paper, but my mind kept wandering back to Paul. We were finally getting along after so much trouble and tension, and it was all going to end. He only had six more months at home before college gobbled him up. It hurt to even think about it. Growing up only sixteen months apart, the times we had been close way outnumbered the difficult times.

And it wasn't just the fact that I was going to miss him, either. I wondered how the house would change when it was just me and my two little sisters. I didn't think Anna would be a problem—she was only eight and was more interested in having fun than just about anything else. Even after Mom's death, she bounced back pretty quickly. But Lucy. She was another issue altogether. She rubbed me wrong sometimes . . . and if I was really honest, I'd have to say I probably bugged her too. She still didn't trust me completely. I didn't blame her for being skeptical, not after all my lies, but still . . . everyone else had given me a chance to get back into their lives and hearts. Lucy was still waiting . . . and watching me. I didn't know how to convince her that I was really serious about God this time, and part of me thought that I shouldn't have to convince her at all. Paul was kind of a nice buffer between us—he seemed to deflect the sparks that sometimes flew. I wondered if those sparks would set off a major bonfire when he left.

"I'm not sure I like this, Beka. You're not going to be around much over the next two months." My dad frowned as he looked at the rehearsal schedule.

"I know, but . . ." I wasn't sure what to say, since I was a little concerned about it too. Not so much the not being at home part. That part was actually good—it would give me time to get my footing with God without so much attention. But I was worried about my classes. I had always been a good student, but it's not like I could just slide my way through. I needed to study and work. Trig and chemistry were hard enough—I enjoyed math and science—but my history and English classes were tough this year too. That's the trouble with getting really good teachers. Good teachers are always twice as hard. And since I had no clue what I wanted to do, I needed to have those grades—Bs weren't an option for some colleges out there. I had kind of blown a lot of my grades last semester when I was depressed and angry and didn't care. I cared now. A lot.

"So," my dad prompted, snapping me out of my thoughts. "What do you want to do about it?"

"I don't know what I can do," I said, sinking into the big blue recliner in the family room. "I mean, I have an actual part and . . . oh, I don't know."

"Do you really want to do this play?"

I covered my face with my hands. "I don't know. Yes, I guess. Maybe." I looked up when Dad laughed. "This isn't funny."

"I know. I don't mean to laugh, but how did you get into this? If you weren't even sure you wanted to do it."

"It seemed like a good idea at the time. And it seemed exciting. But I guess I didn't realize it was going to be such a huge commitment."

"I can understand that." He nodded.

"But I said I'd do it. I ought to follow through with it. Don't you think?"

My dad smiled that warm, soft smile of his and nodded. "Yeah, that sounds about right. But you'll speak up if you feel like you're drowning, right? I know you want to get your grades back up and work on your relationship with God. You will let me know if it all gets to be too much?"

"Sure." I smiled. He seemed satisfied, but I wondered

if I would even recognize I was drowning in time to yell out for help. It probably would have helped if I trusted myself to know when I needed help. Just the fact that I had stayed in a psychiatric hospital—the very thought caused my stomach to flip over—made me feel incompetent somehow. Like there was something wrong with me and it was just hidden better now. In fact, even though I had confessed my big secret, I had almost traded it for a new one. Somehow, Gretchen finding out about Lori's pending adoption made me vulnerable. Could she possibly find out about me—Beka Madison, former psychiatric inpatient?

It didn't help at all that my doctors and family said that I "shouldn't be ashamed of needing help." The shame had wrapped itself around me like a boa constrictor that threatened to choke me if someone found out. And it really wasn't only the hospital. I was going to have to start seeing a counselor. My dad had insisted on it, and at the time, I didn't think much of it. Compared to the hospital, it didn't seem like a big deal. My first appointment was still two weeks away. Dad had said that we needed to get through the holidays and the start of school first. I was pretty sure that he wasn't going to let me back out of it now, though.

Out of pure necessity, I hauled out the rest of my homework, putting off the English paper once again. Mrs. Hollingsworth had asked us to write an essay comparing a book we enjoyed to our own lives—explaining why it impacted us. Normally, I liked assignments like that, but I couldn't even come up with a book to use. I did enjoy reading when I got a spare moment, but I couldn't think of anything that could compare to my crazy life.

*   *   *

At rehearsal the next day, Gretchen was acting particularly smug. I assumed it had to do with her discovery of Lori's secret. She had already let me know that she hadn't found out anything else, but that she wasn't going to give up until she knew the whole story. Knowing Gretchen, part of me wondered if I should warn Lori about what was going to eventually happen.

"There just has to be some story in it . . ." Gretchen stopped talking as I fell into a seat in front of her and Mai.

"I thought you weren't going to say anything, Gretchen." I kept my voice steady despite my nerves.

"Oh, please. Mai isn't just anyone." Gretchen waved her hand at me as if I was being ridiculous.

"Gretchen, front and center." T's voice boomed from the stage, and Gretchen leaped out of her seat, leaving Mai staring at me.

"What?" I finally asked.

"Oh, nothing." Mai smiled in a way that sent the hairs up on my neck. She reached up and twirled a piece of her silky black hair around her finger. We sat there like that for about an eternity, and just as I was about to try to make an exit, she leaned forward. "I would just be careful if I were you."

"What is that supposed to mean?" I almost didn't want to know.

"Well, Gretchen is giving you a chance to prove

yourself. I wouldn't blow it if I were you." She paused and narrowed her eyes. "You're only going to get one shot."

"I still don't know what . . ."

"All orphans onstage." T's voice interrupted my question, and Mai and I both stood and headed for the stage. I let her get as far ahead of me as possible. I really had no idea what she was getting at, but our conversation rattled in my head. Did Gretchen know Mai was going to say those things, or was she acting alone? I felt like throwing up. I didn't need any more complications in my life. Wasn't it complicated enough?

*   *   *

"Hey, Molly, wait up." I smiled before I even turned around. I had only seen Mark from a distance at rehearsals so far, but that was definitely his voice.

"So, how's the orphanage?" Mark asked as he reached my side. I had this sudden urge to reach up and run my fingers through his thick, wavy hair. *Where did that come from?* I wondered.

"Not bad, but it's a lot more work than I expected—I had no idea so much went into a play," I blurted out in one breath. *Slow down,* I thought. *I have to relax.*

"Yeah, it's amazing, isn't it? Too bad we don't have any scenes together. I haven't really gotten to see you."

My thoughts exactly. Out loud I said, "Yeah, they have everybody pretty broken up."

"It won't be like that the whole time."

We reached the parking lot entirely too quickly, but when we got to my car, Mark leaned against the driver's side door. "We haven't really gotten a chance to talk since New Year's."

"I know," I said quietly, unsure of what he might be thinking. I had replayed New Year's Eve a hundred times in my mind, always trying to remind myself that we had agreed to be friends. Friends. For the first time in my life I actually wanted more than that, and it wasn't an option.

"Well, we agreed to be friends, right? Would it be okay if I called you sometime? Friends talk on the phone all the time." He smiled that gentle smile that curled up just a little bit more on the right. It made my heart melt. At that moment, every other thought evaporated. He wanted to call me.

"Sure, I'd like that," I said. I spoke calmly, but on the inside I was leaping.

"Okay then. I just wanted to make sure it was all right with you." He moved away from my door and touched my shoulder before he waved good-bye. "Talk to you later."

I watched him leave before pulling my keys out. I hadn't even noticed it was cold before that moment. I slid into the car. My emotions were so jumbled all of a sudden. Should I have prayed about it before answering? Should I have checked with my dad? It all seemed so simple a second ago, and now I wasn't so sure.

Lord, I really don't know how all this works yet. I want to do what's right. But I really think I like Mark. Please help me. I didn't know what else to pray. So I started my car and headed home. But I found it impossible not to hope that I would get a phone call very soon.

*   *   *

I ate dinner as fast as I could so that I could get back to my room and near my phone. But before I could make my escape, Lucy ruined everything.

"So when are we leaving for youth group?" she asked as we were clearing the dishes.

"What?" I was still distracted, straining to hear the upstairs phone ring.

"Youth group? It starts up again tonight. You are going, right?"

Her tone was rather accusatory, in my opinion, and I squared my shoulders ready to defend myself. "No, I'm not," I answered.

"But you have to take me. Dad said that you were going to drive me."

"Well, I can't. I haven't even finished half of my homework. So you'll just have to get someone else to take you."

"But . . ." she started to say, but then turned and left the kitchen. Two minutes later she returned, my dad in tow.

"What's going on?" he asked.

"Why are you asking me? I'm sure she filled you in." I was only mad at Lucy, but I couldn't keep the anger out of my voice when I answered him.

"I'd like to hear your version."

"My version? I can't take her to youth group. I have homework to do. End of story." I finished wiping the table and tried to leave.

"Wait, Beka. Sit down for a second."

I dropped into one of the chairs with a growl. "I have homework to do. Really."

"I guess I made an assumption," he began. "I thought you would be returning to the youth group now that you are working on your relationship with God."

"Well, we never talked about it. I'm not against going, but I didn't get home till five. I have to finish an English paper, and I still have trig and chemistry homework. There's just no way I can go." I tried to sound reasonable, but it came out all whiny.

"So you're not planning on going at all?" He had that "parental concern" look on his face.

"I don't see how. Unless I don't happen to have homework on a Tuesday night. Which I doubt will ever happen."

"I'm not too happy about this. It's important for you to develop friendships with other Christians and to grow spiritually. Youth group can help you do both of those things."

"Lori's a Christian. I see her." I argued.

"But you both are brand-new. It would be good for you to see young people who are further along."

"So you want me to drop out of the play? I can't do that." My thoughts scrambled around even as I tried to defend staying in the play. My dad was giving me an out, and I was scared to take it. Even though the play itself scared me, I was more scared to try and get out of it.

"I'm not asking you to." He leaned back in his chair and ran his fingers through his hair. "I guess we'll just have to play this one out, and you can go on those nights when you can finish your schoolwork."

"So who's going to take me?" Lucy asked. I didn't realize she had been standing in the doorway the whole time.

"I'll take you." He stood up and headed out of the kitchen. "Why don't you go get ready?"

I took the opportunity to make my escape. As soon as I got to my room, I picked up the phone to hear the stuttering dial tone, letting me know there was a message. My dad had finally caved in and gotten a package from the phone company that gave both lines not only voice mail but also call waiting and caller ID. I loved it, even though I had also been told that I was going to have to share my phone line with Lucy the following year. For now, though, it was still all mine. I held my breath as I dialed to retrieve the message, but it was just Gretchen in a total panic for me to call her back.

I picked up the phone, then put it right back down. I simply didn't have the energy to deal with her.

He didn't call. I found myself rather irritated by the next morning. I mean, if he wasn't going to call, why did he make such a big deal about asking me? I tried to be polite to my family so they wouldn't ask questions about my mood, but Lucy seemed bent on irritating me even more.

"It was a great meeting last night—you should've come," Lucy said the minute she saw me. "It was this guy named Tim. He's from another church up north somewhere I think. He talked about our destinies." She said the word *destinies* as if she was starstruck.

"Yeah, well, I was destined to finish my English paper."

I was glad my dad wasn't in the room. He hates it when we're sarcastic.

Lucy, however, either didn't notice or ignored it, because she just kept talking. "I couldn't sleep last night. I just kept thinking about what God might have planned for me. I mean, I'm glad He's got a plan, but I just can't imagine what it is."

"Who's got a plan?" Anna asked. She bounced into the kitchen and dove into the cereal cabinet.

"God," Lucy answered. "God has a plan for each of us."

"Duh. Even I know that. What's He plannin' for you?" She asked the question but seemed preoccupied with her Cheerios.

"I don't know." Her voice grew quiet, and then she turned her attention back to me. "What do you think God has planned for you?"

"He probably plans for me to get to school today." I shoved a can of lemonade into the side pocket of my backpack and tossed it over my shoulder.

"That's not what I mean." She sighed loudly.

"I know what you mean." But I still didn't answer her question. I didn't feel like thinking about the future. I couldn't seem to handle the present well enough. I started for the door when I heard my dad.

"Leaving already?" he asked.

I turned around. "Yeah, well . . ." I couldn't think of a good excuse to leave so early, so I just stood there feeling awkward.

"We were talking about God's plan for us. You know, that stuff we talked about last night?" Lucy had walked up and given him a hug.

"Yes. Come to any conclusions?" he asked.

"Me? No, not really." She paused long enough for it to seem weird, and then she dropped a bomb. "I was thinking about starting again. You know, gymnastics."

Everybody grew silent and stared at her. Paul walked into the kitchen and looked around.

"What's wrong?" he asked.

"It's me," Lucy said. "I was just telling everyone that I was thinking about starting gymnastics again."

"Really? Lucy, I think that would be wonderful." My dad had recovered from his shock and now grabbed her in a big hug.

"Well, I'm not sure yet. You really think I should?"

"I wish you had never stopped." His voice cracked as if he was holding back tears. It sent my thoughts flying back to the reason Lucy quit gymnastics. Mom. Dad had tried to convince her not to stop, to just take a break and see how she felt, but Lucy had been determined. With everybody focused on Lucy, I slipped out the back door. I felt like I should have been happy for her, but I wasn't. And I couldn't figure out why it was bugging me so much.

*   *   *

"Was she good at it?" Lori asked. I was filling her in on that morning's events, hoping she might have some brilliant insight into why Lucy felt like a thorn in my side.

"Yeah. She was really good. She was already on Level 9." I pushed the corn around on my tray, remembering her last competition.

"What does that mean?"

"Oh, well, there's ten levels that they go through, and then after that there is the elite level—those are the ones trying to get to the Olympics and all that."

"Wow. I had no idea. And you're upset about it?" Lori put her fork down and folded her arms.

"Yeah, sort of. It was her 'thing,' you know? Anna was into horses, even though she just started riding last year. Paul always did sports, especially baseball. And Lucy did gymnastics. Things were always scheduled around her competitions and practices."

"What was your 'thing'?"

"I didn't have a thing. Not really. I guess the butter-flies." I thought about that for a minute. "But that wasn't really a thing. That's not much different than having a garden or collecting dolls. I guess I never had a thing."

"Maybe that's what's bothering you. You don't really have anything that really makes *you* different."

"I don't know. It never bothered me before."

"Yes, but things have changed. You committed to following God. That changes things."

"I forgot to tell you that part. Just before Lucy made her little announcement, that's what she was talking about. God's plan, her destiny, stuff like that."

"God's plan? Like for our lives?"

I nodded. "And you know what? I don't have a clue. I've been wondering about that all morning, when I haven't been annoyed with Lucy, and I don't have any idea about what I'm supposed to do with my life."

"Neither do I. My future always seemed . . . uncer-tain. If God hadn't brought me to the Rollins family, I would have ended up on my own at eighteen. That's only two years away." She shuddered and took a sip of her soda. "I figured I would have to start working and maybe take some college classes if I could afford them. But now everything's changed. I actually have a family who'll support me. It's pretty amazing."

"Yeah, but you at least have some direction. You said you wanted to study different languages and do that international relations stuff. That's at least an idea of what you want to do."

"But I don't know what God wants me to actually do with all that yet. He says He will guide us. We just have to trust Him."

"But I don't even have a clue. Shouldn't I have a clue?"

"I guess. I don't know." Lori shrugged her shoulders and tentatively gathered up her belongings. "Are you going to be okay? You look kind of stressed."

"I'll be fine," I said, trying to add a smile. She looked relieved and hurried off to her next class. I didn't want to admit that my stomach was all twisted up. I walked slowly to fifth period, even though I didn't have much time to get there. I really wanted to go away somewhere and just think. Think about all the things swirling around in my head. Try to make some sense of my life.

My thoughts flickered to Jesus. They were always saying at church how Jesus is a friend—someone who knows all about what we're going through. Someone who is always there for us. I believed it. I wanted to believe it. But somehow, Jesus felt far away. Way up there in the sky somewhere, not walking the halls of Bragg

County. I meant it when I asked Him to come into my heart and even felt His closeness for a while, but now, when my thoughts turned toward Him I had to wonder why He would concern Himself with a sixteen-year-old girl. *Help me, Lord,* I prayed silently. *Help me know that You are here. That I'm not alone in this. Tell me what I'm supposed to do.* Even as I prayed, my thoughts roared so loudly that I wondered how I would even hear God if He answered me.

After a week of rehearsals, I was very nearly in panic mode. Between the rehearsals and homework I barely had time to eat, much less sort out my frustrations over Lucy and Mark. I kept feeling that if he had just called, then I wouldn't have felt so on edge. But I knew that it was more than just Mark, or even Lucy. It was me. I couldn't figure out why I was feeling out of sorts. And as we were driving to church I became more and more tense. I tried to relax, tried to focus on breathing, but I still wanted to jump out of the car and run home. I didn't feel ready to face everybody.

Even though we had gone to church over the holidays, the senior high Sunday school class had not met.

Back when I was going to all the church things, I kept to myself as much as possible, so I never really got to know anyone at church. This would be their first Sunday meeting, and I was going to have to go. I had thought that I might be able to casually ask my dad if I could keep helping out in the nursery, which is where I had hidden for a good part of the last year, but he had made not one but two different comments about hoping I'd enjoy getting involved in the class with the other kids my age. It was his way of making his expectations crystal clear.

When it was time to go to class, I dawdled getting my stuff together and walking down the hallway. I hadn't even made it to the door before I got enveloped by a huge hug. All I could see was red. I thought maybe I had passed out, until the girl leaned back and I could see her face framed with her thick, wild red hair.

"Oh, I'm sorry. Not the hugging type, huh?" The girl smiled and gestured toward my face. "You look shocked."

"Oh, well. I guess not." I wasn't sure what to say.

"Don't worry. She hugs everybody," another girl said as she came up to me from behind. We were all just kind of standing in the hallway, and I really wanted to start walking again, but the two girls seemed in no hurry to get anywhere.

"I'm Nancy," the second girl said with a smile. She was just a little taller than I, with smooth blonde hair and a fashion magazine face. I was surprised by her name, though. Nancy seemed rather old-fashioned—especially when she seemed so fashionable. I didn't think anything had registered on my face, but then she laughed and added, "I know, nobody is named Nancy anymore. My mother was a Nancy Drew fan. Can you believe it? I've forgiven her for it, though." She laughed and smiled again.

"And I'm Allison—the mad hugging monster," the redhead added. She smiled in a friendly way, but she towered over me and I couldn't help but feel a little intimidated.

"We're assuming that you're headed to our class, right? Or Allison accosted you for no reason at all?" Nancy asked. I only got a chance to nod before Allison spoke up.

"We've seen you in church before, just never back here. We're glad you're coming to class. We kind of wondered why you never joined us, but since it's really none of our business, we never asked." She linked her arm through mine, Allison grabbed the other arm, and suddenly we were headed down the hallway again, with Allison still chattering. "We know your name is Beka because of Paul, but we don't know anything about you —well, we know about your mom and all because everybody knew about that."

Nancy reached across and gently pushed at Allison's shoulder. "Could you have any less tact?"

"What?" Allison asked. "She knows about her mom."

"Hel-loooo, Allison. That's not something you just blurt out." Nancy sighed and shook her head.

Allison started to protest again, but I jumped in. "No, really, it's okay."

Nancy grew serious and said, "We were really sorry to hear about that. So tragic."

They both were quiet as we made our way into the senior high room. I stopped in the doorway, because instead of a typical classroom with a couple long tables and chairs, it was set up to look like an outdoor French café. It was incredible. Along one whole wall was a mural of French storefronts. There was a bakery, or Patisserie, the café, which was named La Something, and various other art and pottery stores. Then along the other long wall, there was a landscape view of Paris as if you were looking from somewhere high above the city. Scattered around the room there were small tables with two or three chairs clustered around each one. Several of the tables sported colorful umbrellas. The flower vases on each table gave it an authentic French café feel. Four round tubes went from floor to ceiling in various spots and were painted to look like tree trunks. Paper leaves hung from the ceiling around each one, and the parts of the ceiling that you could see between the "trees" was painted a bright blue. The finishing touch was flooring that looked like cobblestones. I felt like I could have really been in Paris.

"Wow!" was the only word I could form as my two chaperones led me to a table with a bright blue and yellow umbrella. Nancy dragged a chair over from a nearby table, and we all settled in as everybody else was taking their seats.

"Isn't this wild?" Allison said. "Kathy did it over the summer last year. We got to help out with it too."

"Yeah, I'll be happy if I never have to cut out another paper leaf for the rest of my life." Even though it sounded like a complaint, Nancy said it with a good-natured smile.

I was just about to ask who Kathy was when a woman in the front of the room gave a short, loud whistle and gave me my answer.

"Ladies, come on now. Let's settle down and get going. I'm Kathy, for those of you who don't know me. I'm one of the leaders here at Harvest Fellowship." I couldn't tell how old she was, but she seemed young. Even though she was very businesslike, getting us right into the day's topics, I liked her. She was easy to listen to. It had escaped me when we first walked in, but the room only had the senior high girls in it. Allison explained later that the boys were meeting together in another part of the building and that they met separately at least once a month. I only recognized a couple of the other girls—there seemed to be lots of new people since I'd been there. I couldn't decide if that was a good thing or not.

Apparently, the girls' group was in the middle of a study on purity. They were gearing up for some retreat they were having in the spring. I didn't understand everything they discussed, except that basically God wanted us to stay pure. I had never even so much as kissed a guy, much less anything else, so I kind of felt like the topic didn't concern me. Allison participated in the discussion so often that Kathy gently teased her about giving someone else a chance. Nancy followed along in her Bible and took a ton of notes. I began to wonder what in the world she was writing down.

Allison and Nancy tried to get me to join a group going to lunch after church, but I told them I had a lot of homework. That was true, but the real reason was because I had had enough. It went much better than I expected, and nothing happened that was embarrassing, but I still wasn't sure. I wanted time to sort everything out. Too bad time was the one thing I was running short of.

*   *   *

I dreaded the thought of going to rehearsal on Monday, which was scary. If I felt like this now, I didn't know how I was ever going to make it through five more weeks of rehearsals. At least Mark would be there. It was my one consolation.

We had blocked some of the larger scenes the previous week, which basically meant that we all learned where we had to go onstage and when we had to be in a certain spot. But this week the singing rehearsals were beginning. I only had a few solo lines to sing, but I was still nervous about singing in front of people. I didn't know if I was going to be able to make anything come out of my mouth with that many people in the room. My dad, and mom before she died, had always encouraged me to join singing groups and choirs, saying I had a good voice, but I guess I never really believed them.

Thompson called for all the orphans to meet in the band room to practice our songs. I was nervous enough about the singing part, and then Thompson made it worse when he called me forward.

"Beka Madison and Rachel Wise, front and center please."

There were only twenty orphans in the room, but my legs still felt like jelly. I wondered seriously if I was going to be able to stand in front of an entire audience when the show opened. I pushed the thought aside because it made my stomach lurch.

"I need to make some assignments before we go any further in rehearsal. Madison, you will understudy Annie, and Wise will understudy for Molly." He handed each of us some sheet music.

"Annie? You mean I have to be Annie if Gretchen gets sick or something?" I was horrified. "But I don't know if I can . . ."

"Nonsense. You're the right choice. Just learn those extra songs and Annie's lines, pay attention in rehearsals, and you'll be fine. Now go. All right, everybody on your feet." He began pounding out the voice exercises we had learned at the beginning of the rehearsal. I walked back to my place still reeling.

Gretchen smirked when I slipped in next to her. "There's nothing to worry about, Madison. Unless I get run over by a truck, I'm going on. So you won't ever be Annie."

I wasn't sure if she was trying to reassure me or warn me.

When we had a break, I flipped through the script to see how many lines Annie had. I moaned when I saw how many there were. Despite the fact that I assumed Gretchen would die rather than miss a performance, I couldn't very well count on that. I was still going to have to learn it all. I was too scared to tell Thompson I didn't want to do it. It was pitiful. I never realized what a wimp I was.

*   *   *

I told my dad at dinner about the understudy role. He was concerned about how much time it was going to take me, but he told me he thought it was great they thought so much of me. I didn't let on that I didn't want to do it. I thought he might really push me to quit. But my world suddenly got brighter when I checked my voice mail after dinner. I listened to the message four times and only erased it because I didn't want anyone else to hear it.

"Hey, Beka, it's Mark. I guess you're busy or something. I'll try back later."

As if I could get anything accomplished after that. I did open my chemistry book and read the same paragraph a dozen times. Even though I had been waiting, I still jumped when the phone rang. I dove for it, then took a breath before I answered so I wouldn't sound too eager.

"Hello." I instantly tried to figure out if I sounded too eager. *Definitely too eager.*

"Hello, is this Beka?" Mark's voice came over the line.

"Yeah. Hi, Mark. What's up?" *Casual. Think casual.*

"How'd you know it was me?" he asked.

Because you are the only male who could have possibly asked for me. Instead I answered, "Umm, I'm good at voices?"

He laughed and I relaxed a tiny bit. "So, how's rehearsal going for you?"

"I don't know. It's all so intense. I had no idea you theater people were such masochists."

"Yeah, we love to torture ourselves for weeks in order to give six performances. It's pretty sad, really."

"Well, this may be my first show, but it will probably also be my last."

"Really? You might want to wait until after the performances to decide that. There's nothing like being on-stage and playing to an audience," he said.

"Yeah, well, that's part of my problem. I'm not sure what will happen when there's a whole audience full of people staring at me. What if I freeze? What if I throw up?" I cringed. *Maybe I shouldn't have added that.*

"You'll do great. I'll be there to help you."

I literally felt my heart begin to pound when he said those words. "Well, thanks," I squeaked out.

"Oh, and I heard about your understudy role. Congratulations."

"Yeah. But I'm sure I won't be doing it. It's Gretchen after all."

"You never know."

That wasn't exactly what I wanted to hear. We chatted for a few more minutes, and then we said good-bye. I kept thinking about his offer to help. It sounded so sweet and so sincere. I didn't even bother trying to talk myself out of daydreaming about him. I didn't want to be his friend. I wanted more than that. *Oh, Lord, help my heart. I want this to be okay with You.*

Mark's phone call kept me floating the rest of the week. I had told Lori about it, trying not to sound too excited. Lori said she was happy for me but told me that I shouldn't get too wound up in him yet. I knew in my head that she was right, but it was too late for my heart. I did try to take her advice, though. She had encouraged me to just watch him and see what he was like, since I didn't really know him very well. But when I watched him at rehearsals, I found myself daydreaming about his voice, his smile, and what it would be like if I were his. I tried to tell myself to take it easy. *Yeah, right, like that is going to work.*

When I told Gretchen on Friday during a break in

rehearsal about him calling me, she had a completely different reaction. One that I was secretly hoping for.

"Why didn't you tell me earlier?" she asked, giving my shoulder a shove.

"I've been busy. I didn't think about it." That wasn't really true. I had been thinking about it every second. "It's no big deal." *Sure, Beka. Keep telling yourself that.*

"We can't miss this opportunity, Beka. We have to start strategizing. There's no time to lose either. It's only eight weeks till the Spring Formal."

"The formal? Strategizing? Gretch, he just called me; he didn't ask me out or anything. You've lost your mind."

"Please, Beka." Her voice took on a parental tone. "How much experience have you had in the dating department? Really?"

I glanced around to see who could hear her. Mai was nearby but seemed to be reading. No one else seemed to hear the statement.

"You wanna keep your voice down, Gretchen? I'd like to not call attention to my pathetic dating history."

"No worries, Beka. I mean, it's not like people don't know you haven't had a boyfriend."

"Gretchen! Give me a break. You make it sound like I'm the only one. Plenty of girls in this school don't have boyfriends."

"Yeah, well."

She didn't continue, but I knew what she was thinking. Anybody who was important and popular in the school did have boyfriends. I had never felt so backward in my life. One more thing that had never bothered me before now suddenly loomed larger than life.

Gretchen moved the subject back to the formal. "Anyway. As I was saying, we have a lot to do. Let's see. Hey, Mai." She waited for Mai to look up and then asked, "Tomorrow night? My house?" Mai gave her a thumbs-up sign. "Good. Now all we have to do is get Liz on board and we'll be ready."

"Ready for what?" I was almost afraid to ask.

"Operation Rooster." Rooster was Mark's name in the play. She continued, "We'll all get together at my house on Saturday night. You all can spend the night so that we have more time. I'm sure Mark likes you. We just need to find a way to encourage him to not be a slug about it."

I didn't argue. There was no point in arguing with Gretchen. But going over to Gretchen's house was going to require a long talk with my dad. One that I was not looking forward to. Plus, I didn't know what Gretchen might be planning in that devious head of hers. Whatever it was, I had a feeling I was going to end up feeling humiliated. But if it got me Mark, maybe it would be worth some humiliation.

*   *   *

I waited until after Lucy had gone to bed to approach my dad.

"Can we talk?" I asked as I crawled into the recliner.

"Sure," he said, slipping off his glasses and putting aside his Bible. "What's on your mind?"

"Well, I got invited to a sleepover tomorrow night. At Gretchen's."

"Gretchen?" he asked. "Would this be the same Gretchen you were out all night with?"

I nodded.

"Tell me what you think."

I hated to talk first. "Well, it really is a sleepover. I'm not lying or anything. It's just a girl thing, some girls from the play. It's a harmless sleepover. That's all."

"Are any of these girls believers?"

"No. But they're not *bad* per se. They're really just typical teenage girls."

"It's not a question of good or bad, Beka. It's a question of influence. You've said that you don't have any time for youth group, and you even canceled going to Lori's house for the last two Wednesdays for that Bible study. I'd rather you spend your free time with people who will help you get to know God and His ways. Gretchen won't be able to help you do that. She's already demonstrated that she makes poor choices."

"Are you telling me I can only hang out with Christians? Dad, these girls are my friends . . . sort of . . . and I have to see them every day and every afternoon."

"That's not what I'm saying exactly. You need to be careful when you're friends with people who don't love God. Especially at first."

"What about 'love your neighbor' and all that? Maybe I'll be a positive influence on them," I argued.

"Maybe you will—someday. But do you feel sure enough about what you believe to resist the wrong things they choose to do? You're just getting started, Beka."

"Are you saying I can't go? Do you remember *at all*

what high school is like? I may never get asked again if I don't go."

"I'm not so sure that would be a bad thing."

"Great. So I become a Christian and my social life has to end? You said you were going to start trusting me to make some decisions. I want to go to this sleepover." I knew I had drawn a line in the sand. I just wasn't sure how far he was willing to go.

He ran his fingers through his hair and then leaned back on the sofa. He didn't say anything for several minutes. I was about ready to make another point when he spoke. "Look, Beka. The fact that you are sixteen means that you are making lots of decisions every day. And you are going to have to learn to take responsibility for those decisions. Apparently you'll be spending time with Gretchen because of the play no matter what you do Saturday night, but I would prefer you not spend any more time with her than necessary."

I began to protest, but he held up a finger. "Wait, I'm not finished. That being said, I will leave the decision up to you. But if I feel, at any time, that I need to step in — I will. And that could mean the end of your friendship with Gretchen. You need to be careful, Beka. I know you see it as harmless, but it's not. Because I love you, I'll be watching."

"Are you trying to make this harder for me? If I decide to go, I get pressure from you, and if I don't go, I get pressure from them. I can't win." I pushed myself out of the chair, figuring there was nothing else to say.

"A little pressure can be a good thing, Beka. Decisions like these shouldn't be taken lightly."

I said good night and left. At least if he had said no, I could have blamed it on him. It was only a sleepover. And he was acting like it was the most important decision of my life. But I didn't really have a choice. I was going to that sleepover. I would just have to deal with him watching my every move. I was suddenly very glad I wasn't at home much anymore.

*   *   *

Dad didn't say much as I left for Gretchen's house Saturday night. He didn't have to, since I knew exactly what he was thinking. I wanted to say something to reassure him that everything was going to be fine, but I wasn't so sure myself.

Gretchen and I had a difficult past. Even though we seemed to be friends now, I knew that could disappear in a moment if I did something that Gretchen didn't like. And life didn't go well if you were on Gretchen's bad side. I had been on that bad side for several months until just before Christmas break last year.

We had actually been friends in middle school, going to each other's houses and all that. Back then she was pretty harmless, but once we hit high school she became more popular and it went to her head. We still got along okay for a while, but at that point I was trying to make my family believe that I was a Christian when I really wasn't. Gretchen tried to pull me into the popular crowd by inviting me to things, but I always said no, and eventually she stopped asking me. After my mother died in March, she was sympathetic for a while, but apparently she felt I was getting too much attention. Things didn't get bad until last fall. She started making nasty comments, and everybody who was near her joined in. I ignored them at school, but I still felt alienated. Then suddenly she asked me to try out for the play and did this 180-degree turnaround. I had been skeptical at first, but so far, everything had been okay.

*   *   *

Gretchen's mother let me in and sent me down to the basement. I kind of wished I hadn't been the first to get there, but I didn't think I could just sit in the car and wait. Besides, after Mai's comments the other day, I didn't want to run into her without Gretchen around. The basement had been turned into a rec room and had couches, a large TV, and even a pool table.

"Gretchen?" I didn't see her anywhere, but her mother had said she was down here.

It was just a minute or so before she appeared from around a corner, wiping her hands on a towel. I couldn't have been more shocked when I saw her.

"Gretchen! What did you do?"

"What? Oh, this." She pulled on one of her curls, which had gone from blonde to bright red since yesterday.

"Yes, that. Why did you dye your hair?" I was still shocked, trying to get used to seeing her look completely different.

"Well, duh. Why do you think I did it?" She crossed the room and flopped onto the couch.

"They have a wig for you to wear. You didn't have to dye it. And you certainly didn't have to dye it a month before the play."

She looked amused. "Oh, Beka. I'm an actress. I have to be as authentic as possible."

*   *   *

Mai and Liz had reactions like mine when they arrived. Gretchen seemed pleased with the shock value of it all. I tried to steer clear of Mai, but it was pretty hard with only four of us there. For a while, everything was fine. Gretchen had rented a video, so we watched that, ate pizza, and chatted about the play and the rehearsals. Gretchen's parents came down to see if we needed anything and to say good night. I was beginning to think that I was home free when Gretchen called us all over to sit on the floor. She shut off the TV and then went and got something out of a drawer in the end table.

"I have something here that will change our lives," she said as she sat down on the floor with us. I was immediately worried.

Mai and Liz leaned forward eagerly.
Gretchen responded by lowering her voice even more.

"I have been waiting for the right time to share this
with you." She leaned back and nodded. "I think the
time is right."

I almost laughed. I wanted to tell her to quit being so
dramatic about it, but Mai and Liz seemed to be buying
the whole routine. So I didn't say anything. I just waited
for Gretchen to get on with it.

After a few more "mysterious" comments, Gretchen
finally showed us what she had.

"These," she said as she held out a deck of cards, "will
tell us our futures." When nobody responded, she added,

"You want to know your future, don't you?" Liz and Mai nodded like robots. I didn't nod; I just stared. They were tarot cards. I had heard about tarot cards but had never seen a deck up close.

"But before we start we have to set the mood." Gretchen leaped up and pulled several plastic bags out from behind the TV. "Here, Liz, light these in each corner of the room." She handed her one of the bags. Gretchen then pulled a pack of incense, matches, and a clay platelike thing from another bag.

"We'll light the incense, and once Liz has the candles all lit we can start." She smiled directly at me and handed me the matches. "Beka, why don't you do the honors?"

I hesitated. It all just felt wrong.

"C'mon, Beka. It's incense, not a snake. Go ahead." Gretchen pushed the matches into my hand. I glanced at Mai. She was waiting to see what I would do. Her words at the rehearsal came back to me. *"You've got one chance. I wouldn't blow it."*

So I lit the incense. I didn't know what else to do. Liz came back and took her place, and Gretchen poured the cards out of the box and began to shuffle them.

"Do you know how to do this?" Liz asked. She sat with her arms wrapped around her knees. Her long blonde hair was pulled back into a ponytail, and in that space I could see her as an individual person—not just as one of Gretchen's lot. She seemed a little concerned. Maybe if she didn't want to do it, I'd get off the hook too.

"I have a cousin who is a Wiccan. Her name is Michelle, but she calls herself Astrid." Gretchen's words picked up tempo as she got more excited. "She gave me the tarot cards a couple of weeks ago and a book about them. Plus, she told me about all of these sites on the Internet that I've been checking out. She told me that I needed to find out more because I'm 'sensitive.' That means I can tap into the forces around me. I'm also able to read subconscious thoughts more easily."

Liz shook her head. "Wiccan? Isn't that witchcraft? I don't know, Gretchen."

I felt the urge to jump in, especially since I wouldn't be the only dissenter. "Yeah, Gretchen, do you really think this is a good idea?"

"Oh, please, Beka. You're not going to get all religious on me now, are you?" Gretchen sighed.

"No, I just, well . . ."

"Look, it's completely harmless. I even saw some Christian tarot cards advertised online, so it's perfectly okay. Besides, my family goes to church too, and my mom was with me when I bought all this stuff. She didn't have a problem with it."

I didn't know how to argue with her. But it still felt all wrong inside.

Gretchen seemed to be losing her patience. "Look, we're all here to help you. Wouldn't God want you to know some of your future, so you know what to do?"

"I'm not sure that's the way . . ."

"Let me just do this and you'll see." She jumped in before I could even finish the thought in my head. She continued, "And all that stuff that says witchcraft is about worshiping Satan and all that is a lie, if that's what you're worried about. Trust me. I read a lot about it. Wiccans don't even believe in Satan. It's mostly about honoring the earth and its forces and stuff. Now, you have to concentrate with me. Concentrate on the cards. Here, close your eyes and shuffle the cards."

* * *

I woke up the next morning feeling like I had been run over by a truck. Gretchen had kept us up most of the night telling our future. She didn't really say anything that seemed dangerous, but my stomach still felt knotted up. I couldn't help but wonder what my dad would say. But still, Gretchen hadn't said anything against God, and she seemed to know a lot about it. She swore us all to secrecy, telling us that if we broke confidence it would come back on us threefold.

Even with the threefold thing, I had the sense that I should talk to my dad about it. But I was scared he would overreact before I even had a chance to explain. I figured I could handle it on my own.

* * *

I had promised my dad that I would meet them at church the next morning. Gretchen was irritated that I wasn't staying, but I was glad for the excuse to leave. I slipped into the row next to Anna just as they began to play the music. Since I had really asked Jesus into my heart, I always felt closest to Him when the music was playing. A calmness would wash over me. But today I couldn't focus. I kept wondering if I was even supposed to worship Him after last night, and I felt guilty, even though I wasn't totally sure why. And I wasn't sure what to do. Praying sounded like the right thing to do, but putting all my thoughts into words was hard sometimes. *Lord, I'm sorry if I did something wrong. I want to understand You better. Help me to know what You want me to do.*

I didn't know if that prayer was good enough, but since I didn't know what else to do, I just closed my eyes and tried to let the music seep into my soul.

When the music stopped and it was time to go to class, Nancy and Allison appeared at my side from out of nowhere.

"Hey, Beka!" Allison said loudly enough to cause the two rows of people in front of us to turn and look. Allison, on the other hand, didn't notice or didn't care.

"You coming to class today?" Nancy asked. When I nodded she added, "Good. I'm glad we didn't scare you off. Allison can be rather alarming." She grinned and poked Allison in the side. Allison snorted and poked her back.

"We're meeting all together today. They have to talk to all of us about the retreat. Are you going to go? Oh, I hope you do. It's so much easier to get to know people at retreats than it is on Sunday mornings." Nancy seemed to genuinely want to get to know me. I liked her. Allison actually was a little much for me, but Nancy was more my speed. Allison saw somebody else she knew and sprinted away from us. Nancy shook her head but smiled.

"I'm not sure. Is this the one you were talking about last week? Something about purity?" I knew my dad would want me to go, but being thrown together for four days with a bunch of kids I didn't know seemed rather terrifying to me.

"Yeah, they have it in the mountains. There's a beautiful lake, but it'll be too cold to swim in April," Nancy said.

"April? Oh, it's over spring break?" I wouldn't be able to use the play as an excuse because that would finish in March.

"Yes. They really wanted us to have more time—usually we just have weekend retreats, but they're over almost as soon as they start. So, do you think you'll go?" Nancy asked again.

"My dad will probably make me go. But I'm not sure I see the point, for me anyway. I don't even have a boyfriend or anything."

Nancy was all over that. "But purity is more than just a boy-girl thing. It's about keeping our hearts pure and all that. Besides, it's better to decide where your boundaries are before you have a guy in your life. We don't always make good decisions in the heat of the moment, so if you know beforehand what you're comfortable with, well, it's just easier to stick to." We reached the doorway to the classroom, but she didn't go in. She leaned against the doorjamb. "Go ahead and ask me."

"Ask you what?" I had no idea what she was talking about.

"Ask me where my boundaries are." She waited with a half smile on her face.

"Isn't that . . ." I glanced around at all the kids nearby. "Well, isn't that kind of private?"

"Not to me. I don't mind talking about it." She must

have figured I wasn't going to ask, because she told me anyway. "I don't have a problem with handholding or sitting close or even a peck on the cheek, but I don't even want to kiss a guy until we're at least engaged."

"You're kidding." I couldn't form any other words. And I wasn't sure how to fit this new information in with what I had already seen about her. She seemed to be really friendly and genuine. She seemed comfortable with who she was. And she seemed to really care about others. I couldn't help but like her, and other people seemed to feel the same way. Gretchen would have said she was a complete prude, but I always saw a prude as someone who was stuck up about his or her opinions, which Nancy wasn't.

"It's true—see." She stuck out her hand and pointed to a ring on her left hand.

"What's that?" I asked.

"It's a purity ring. My dad gave it to me when I was fourteen. It shows that I am committed to God to stay pure until I get married."

"Don't other kids . . . well, don't people think that's weird?" I couldn't help but ask.

She didn't seem to mind the question. "Honestly, I don't care if they think I'm weird. And the word other kids usually use is 'crazy.'" She grinned. "Maybe I am, I don't know. But I've got to do what I think is right. That's why you should go with us on the retreat. It'll help you figure out where your boundaries are. And, of course, it will give us a chance to hang out together." She glanced down at her hands, then looked at me. "Oh, speaking of that, there's a concert Saturday night here at the church.

A couple of other girls are spending the night with me afterwards. Why don't you come too? It'll be a blast, I promise."

"Well, I, uh . . ." Just then we heard a voice bellow from inside the classroom.

"C'mon people. Let's get going."

"You think about it," Nancy said. "We better get in there." She pulled my elbow as we made our way into the café. The chairs at the tables were all filled, so we found a spot on the floor. Once again, I recognized a few faces but most of them were unfamiliar. Paul was there too, talking with a couple guys at one of the tables. I gave him a small wave when he looked over and saw me. We waited while everyone settled down.

I was awfully glad we got interrupted. I needed time to think about the invitation. I thought I probably should go. But it made me nervous, even more nervous than when I went over to Gretchen's. Nancy was pretty secure with her relationship with God, and I figured the other girls would be too. I still felt like a preschooler. There was so much I didn't understand. I didn't even know about that purity ring stuff. I felt like I needed to figure out more about God so that I wouldn't say something completely stupid. I went back and forth in my mind during the whole class. I barely heard what they were saying about the retreat. They gave us a brochure about the retreat with a registration form to fill out. I took one and shoved it in my Bible. I could only deal with one decision at a time. And I was sure Nancy would call very soon looking for an answer.

At Monday's rehearsal, I came with my camera in tow. I was doing double duty since the yearbook wanted some rehearsal pictures and *The Bragg About*, the school newspaper, was running a story on the play the following week. When I wasn't in a scene, I'd slip out into the audience or into one of the wings to snap pictures. I really tried not to snap too many of Mark, but I found myself aiming the camera at him whenever I could. I only got profiles though, because when he turned to look at me, I'd turn or pretend I was checking something. I decided I'd have to develop the pictures myself, since I didn't want anyone to see the whole roll.

I was trying to get a shot of some of the orphans

when Gretchen dragged my arm and pulled me into the hallway. My mind was swimming with everything I was trying to do—taking the pictures, rehearsing my own part, and still trying to learn Gretchen's part—and I was mad that she couldn't wait until after rehearsal. It was so typical. Gretchen always came first. I didn't get a chance to even speak before she dove in.

"So! What did you think?"

"Huh? About what?"

"The tarot cards, you dope. Your fortune?" she whispered. "What did you think? You ran off before we could talk."

"Oh, I don't know. It was cool I guess."

"Yeah, but what did you think about what I told you about Mark?" She was groping for a reaction from me, but I didn't oblige.

"What? You just said that romance was in my future. That could mean years from now, and it doesn't mean Mark."

"But remember what I told you my cousin said? That I'm 'sensitive.' I just know that you and Mark are destined to be together. We took longer with the tarot cards than I wanted, so we didn't have time . . ." She stopped when we heard T's voice in the auditorium. We stood silently for a minute, listening to see if we needed to be onstage. When we realized he was calling for a scene we weren't in, she continued. "I didn't get a chance to show you the spells."

"Spells? Gretchen, how deep into this are you? First you're doing all this fortune-telling, and now you're talking about casting spells? I don't know about this."

"Look. I told you already that Wicca isn't about Satan or anything. Wiccans aren't supposed to hurt anybody with their magic. It's in their law. Anyway, I have a spell we could try on Mark."

"No way, Gretchen. We can't do that to him. Besides, it's not the same if you make someone like you. Not that I'm sure you can do that anyway."

"Oh, please, it will be fine. But spells work best with three. So I thought you, Mai, and me can get together this weekend. Saturday night again."

Are you deaf? "I don't know, Gretchen."

Her voice morphed from friendly to fierce. "Look, Beka. This is all to help you. Quit being so stuck-up about it."

T's voice interrupted again, and this time we had to get onstage.

Her voice still threatening, she added, "You want me to be your friend, don't you?" She changed her tone again when I nodded. She returned to being friendly. "Good. Then friends help each other out."

We left to go back onstage, but now instead of the play swirling around in my head, it was Gretchen, spells, and an image I imagined of what a Wiccan would look like.

Besides, the fact that Mai would be there without even Liz as a buffer bothered me almost as much as what Gretchen wanted to do. But I also knew what was in store for me if I refused. Gretchen would make life miserable for me at school. If she turned against me and started casting spells on me . . . I shuddered. I didn't know if spells worked at all, much less her spells, but it still bothered me. I was glad to have a social life again, but it was like walking a tightrope. Saturday night left me with a choice between spells with Mai and Gretchen or Nancy's "God girls" get-together. What was I supposed to do? Obviously, God would probably want me to go to Nancy's. But if I did, what would Gretchen do to me? It was just too much to deal with.

*   *   *

The next day, I thought about asking Lori what she thought I should do, but I knew what her answer would be. Besides, at lunch the next day she was fairly bouncing with excitement.

"I couldn't wait to talk to you today. I went somewhere last night." She grinned and tucked her long, dark curls behind one ear. I guessed she was waiting for me to ask.

"Okay, where'd you go?"

"I took a dance class. I've never danced in my life, but I really loved it." She launched into the story without waiting for me to prod her. "When we were in church on Sunday, we found out about a dance class that the church was offering. So I went and I loved it. I'm not any good at it yet, but since it's all about worship, praising God, it doesn't really matter. It makes me feel close to Him. Like I'm honoring Him. It was awesome."

"I think I saw something like that at our church a couple of years ago. But I didn't realize it was worship." Lori had the slender frame of a dancer, so I could imagine her at a dance class like that.

"Yeah. There's a Scripture. Wait. I wrote it down somewhere." She bent down and dug in her backpack. She pulled out a small notebook. "Here it is. It's Psalm 149:3, 'Let them praise his name with dancing.' There are other Scriptures too. I think it's something I really want to do. So you all don't have dance classes at your church anymore?"

"No. I've never heard of any."

"You don't have to belong to our church to go to the classes. Do you maybe want to come to a class with me?"

"I don't think so. I mean, it sounds great and all, but dancing isn't my thing. I have to do it in the play, but it's all choreographed with a group of us."

"Your thing. Have you found your 'thing,' yet?" She took another bite of her burger while she waited for me to answer.

"To be honest, I've hardly had time to think. This play takes up so much time, and then with my homework—it's my whole life right now. Gretchen is always quoting, 'Drama is my life; I have no choice. Drama is my choice; I have no life.' But not me. This will be my big debut and finale all rolled into one."

"Yeah, you have been kind of busy. When does this play happen anyway?"

"The second and third weekend of March. I couldn't believe it when I saw the schedule. Our opening night is the same night my mom . . ." I couldn't finish the sentence. But I could tell that Lori understood.

"Well, maybe it's good that you'll have so much going on that night, and the nights leading up to it. It'll get easier. I promise."

And she should know. She lost her father and her

mother less than a year apart. Even though Lori was so supportive about my mom dying, it always felt a little pathetic when I compared my tragedy to hers. At least I still had a father. And he adored me even though he could be a little overinvolved at times.

"After the play is over, will you be able to come to the Bible study at my house? There's another girl at my church that wants to come too. She's going to come tomorrow to check it out."

So Lori had made another friend. I knew it would happen, even hoped it would happen, but I still felt a stab of jealousy when she said someone else was going. Megan, Lori's foster mother, had helped both Lori and me learn about Jesus. She wanted to help us get on the right track with our walks, so she had suggested a Bible study group to meet at her house. Because of the play, I hadn't been able to go. Now I wasn't sure I wanted to. But I didn't want to say anything to Lori about not wanting another girl to meet with her, so I just told her that I would have to wait until my hectic life calmed down. She seemed satisfied. I felt exhausted. Having no friends was lonely, but it certainly was easier than juggling them so that they didn't all collide together.

*   *   *

I was forced into making a decision about Saturday before I had even had time to think about it. After dinner Tuesday night, and after Paul had taken Lucy to youth group, my dad asked me to come talk with him in the family room.

I followed him in there nervously. I hadn't really done anything wrong, and he couldn't know about the Gretchen thing, so I wasn't sure why I was nervous. Maybe because he seemed so serious. I perched on the edge of the couch and waited.

"First of all, I wanted you to know that I wasn't going through your things. I promise. But you left your Bible on the kitchen table on Sunday, and when I moved it I saw this sticking out of it." He pulled the purity retreat brochure out of the Bible. "They've mentioned this retreat in church, so I did know about it, but I didn't want to push it on you. Then I saw this, and I just really felt like we should talk about it. So, what do you think? Do you want to go?"

I shrugged. "I don't know. I guess I'd feel funny about going. All those kids know each other and stuff."

"But you said that you had made some friends, didn't you?"

"Yeah, they're nice, but it's not like I know them really well or anything." He didn't say anything for a moment. Then I added, "You want me to go, don't you?"

He stayed silent for another minute and then let out a breath he had been holding. "Yes, I suppose I do. But I'm not going to force you if you don't want to. I know it would be a bit of a stretch, since you've never been, but that might be good for you."

"I'll think about it, but I'm not making any promises." I wasn't even sure I wanted to think about it.

"Fair enough. Let me know what you decide before this is due, okay?"

"While we're here I needed to ask you something." The words came flying out before I could stop them.

"Sure. What's on your mind?"

"Can I go out on Saturday night? I got invited . . . somewhere." I had to say something, but as soon as the words were out of my mouth, I wanted to take them back. He was going to want to know the details of both invitations. If I had waited until after I knew where I wanted to go, then I could have just told him about the one invitation. I felt like an idiot.

"You want to be more specific?"

I knew it. My mind raced. Where should I go? Going to Nancy's would please my dad. Going to Gretchen's would please, well, Gretchen. I had to make a quick decision.

"Oh, it's just a sleepover at Nancy's house. I guess she invited some other girls too." I felt like smacking myself on the forehead. What was I thinking? Now I'd actually have to go to Nancy's. Something in me made me say the one thing that would make my dad happy.

And it worked. A slow smile spread across his face. "Nancy? The girl you met at church?"

I just nodded. What was I thinking?

"Sure. That sounds great. Maybe it will help you decide about the retreat too."

I nodded again. I couldn't speak. Talk about impulsive. I should have just waited until I had figured things out, and now I was stuck. After I went to my room, I stared at my phone for probably half an hour before I got up the nerve to call Gretchen. I knew Nancy would eventually call me, so I didn't need to call her, but telling

Gretchen over the phone would be easier than telling her in person. She could be rather intimidating.

I dialed. Gretchen answered. "Hello?"

"Hey, Gretch. It's me."

"I'm glad you called." She was all business. "We're going to have to come up with another time to do our get-together. Mai's going to her grandparents' or some lame thing this weekend, so we'll have to wait."

"Oh, that's too bad." *Yeah, too bad.*

"Yeah, so we'll figure something out for next week. Besides, it'll give me some more time to do some research."

"Research?"

"Yeah, I found some really cool Wicca sites that tell you all about it. You can even ask questions and stuff. You know, I was thinking about starting a coven."

"Coven? What are you talking about?"

"A coven. A group of witches. We already have four with you, Liz, Mai, and me—but I think you're supposed to have thirteen. Keeping anything a secret in this town is hard enough, so maybe the fewer people we have, the better. We should at least ask Theresa, maybe Chrissy if she stops hanging out with those losers she calls friends. What do you think?"

"Honestly? I think you've lost your mind. Are you seriously talking about being a witch?" I was surprised at myself for being so blunt, but Gretchen didn't miss a beat.

"It's not crazy, Beka. There's a lot of people out there who do it."

"So? There's a lot of people who murder people too."

"It's like a religion without the rules. You are just supposed to be good and kind and take care of nature and be responsible for your own actions. Now, does that sound bad?"

"No, not really. But it's a cult. I know that much."

"Oh, Beka." That condescending tone was back in her voice. "Christianity is more of a cult than Wicca."

"What?" I wanted out of this conversation but I couldn't help myself.

"Cults follow a person, and Christianity follows Jesus. Wicca doesn't follow anybody. You do what is right for you. Nobody dictates who you worship or how you do it. Some of them pray; some of them don't. They don't even all use magic. It's up to the individual. I think it sounds great."

She was making it sound like it was perfectly harmless, good even, but in my gut I still knew it was wrong. The problem was I didn't know why, so I couldn't even argue with her. I decided changing the subject would be smarter.

"So, who do you think will be the editor next year?" I asked.

Gretchen and I were both on the newspaper staff. It was called *The Bragg About*, and kids were already talking about who would be the new editor in the fall. It was always a senior, and I was secretly hoping it would be me. I wasn't necessarily the best writer, but I was good at fixing other people's writing, and it would give me a chance to do more photography and design. It had crossed my mind that maybe that was my "thing" since I loved taking photos. Being the newspaper editor sounded like a good way to find out.

"Well, obviously Ms. Adams is going to choose the most qualified person. She's crazy if she doesn't choose me. I'd obviously be the most qualified. And I can get anybody to talk about anything. I always have the inside scoop."

Whoops. Maybe I should have picked a different subject.

"I didn't know you wanted to be editor." I chose not to add my opinion that she'd be a lousy editor. She was too bossy, and she'd turn the paper into one big gossip column. I decided not to say that either.

"Well, it's the only way the paper is going to have any class. Can you imagine if that nerdy Olive gets it?"

"Olive's nice."

"You think everybody's nice."

Not true. It's not how I would describe you.

I decided getting off the phone was the safest thing to do. Mai had made things easy for me, but I didn't want to press my luck.

"I better go and study for chemistry. I bet he'll give a pop soon."

"Oh, we're having one tomorrow. Ten questions. It's on the stuff in chapter 8—study the book, not your notes, though."

"How do you know? We're not supposed to know about pop quizzes. Hence the word 'pop.'"

"Oh, Beka." There it was again. "Don't you know by now that I have sources everywhere?"

The thought made me shudder. But even so, after I got off the phone I pushed my notebook aside and pulled out my chemistry book instead. No sense in not taking the advice.

Even though the play was unrelenting, I kind of felt like I was managing. I was mostly concerned about looking stupid with Nancy and all her friends on Saturday night. But then Thursday came.

And on Thursday, everything went haywire.

Lori was the first one to tell me. She found me at my locker even before classes started.

"You'll never believe what happened yesterday!"

"What?" I was preoccupied looking for my history folder in the bottom of my locker.

"Well, I went to this interest meeting for the yearbook committee and . . ."

"You're going to do yearbook? That's great! I take

photos for the yearbook. Well, I take them when I'm not up to my ears in rehearsals."

"Oh, good. It'll be fun to work on it together."

"Well, what happened?" I asked.

"Oh yeah. Well, this guy asked me out. I said no, of course, but it was just bizarre that he came up out of the blue like that."

I wasn't surprised. Lori was very pretty, and I had seen more than one guy look twice at her. The thought crossed my mind that maybe I should hang out with people who were more average looking.

"Who was it?"

"Jerry? No, it was Jeremy."

"Jeremy Carpenter?" My throat was so tight I could barely get the words out.

"Yeah, you know him?"

"You could say that. He's Gretchen's boyfriend." The reality of what that meant was only beginning to register. Lori, however, seemed unfazed.

"Why would he ask me out if he's got a girlfriend? Well, it doesn't matter anyway since I said no. He's pretty full of himself. When he asked me out he actually told me what kind of car he drove. As if that would make a difference." Lori laughed and then glanced at her watch. "I better get to class. See you in second." She waved as she went down the hallway.

I leaned my head on my locker door and knocked it gently a few times. I couldn't believe it. It wouldn't take long for word to get back to Gretchen about it. And when she found out she would be furious. Unfortunately for Lori, she wouldn't be angry with Jeremy. No, I knew exactly who she was going to blame.

"C'mon. It can't be that bad," a voice said behind me.

I turned to see who it was and almost smacked my nose on Mark's chest. I stepped back and said, "What can't be that bad?"

"You're banging your head on your locker." He reached up and touched my forehead. "I figured something must be wrong." He moved his hand down to my shoulder and smiled the kind of smile that turned my insides into a puddle.

"Oh, well, Lori just had some news that could potentially ruin her life. Only she doesn't know it yet."

"Sounds serious." He settled himself against the locker and folded his arms across his chest.

The bell rang. *That wretched bell. Why couldn't I have gotten five more minutes? Just five more minutes.*

"I guess we'll have to continue this later. Do you want to grab some dinner after rehearsal tonight?"

"Umm." *Okay, mouth, work, please work.* "I thought . . . I mean . . ." I couldn't formulate thoughts or words.

"Don't stress. It's just dinner. I mean, it's not like a date or something."

Stupid me.

"Oh, well, sure. I guess." I was embarrassed but not embarrassed enough to actually say no.

"Good, then we'll catch up then." He squeezed my shoulder and left me standing there. As soon as he was out of sight, I melted against my locker. I was late for class. And I couldn't care less.

*   *   *

75

Since Gretchen and Lori were both in my second period English class, I walked very slowly as I made my way there. I turned into the classroom, and one look at Gretchen's face gave me my answer. She knew. She was staring at the blackboard so fiercely I half expected it to burst into flames. Lori was already sitting two rows behind Gretchen—I was glad I had missed her entrance.

I barely heard what Miss Hanson said, since the tension in the room was suffocating. Of course, probably no one else even noticed. I doodled on my notebook as I thought about how to escape the disaster ahead. When the bell rang, Gretchen stormed out of class, making me suspect that she might come after me too, since Lori was my friend.

And I was right.

Our seventh period journalism class was divided into two parts; the first part we worked as a class, and during the second part we wrote and designed *The Bragg About*. As soon as Ms. Adams released us to work on the paper, Gretchen made a beeline for my desk. Her eyes were definitely red, which surprised me. It made Gretchen seem almost human. I had imagined her angry, not hurt. But I only felt sorry for her for a moment.

"How could you?" she burst out when she reached my desk.

"How could I what? I didn't do anything. Gretchen, you can't blame me for something Jeremy did." I knew I was on the defensive, but I couldn't help it.

"Why didn't you tell that . . . that . . . thing that Jeremy was off limits?"

"There was no reason to. She didn't go after him. She's not even interested."

"Why not? What's wrong with Jeremy?"

"What?" *Now she's mad that Lori's not interested?* "Gretchen, you're losing it."

Gretchen looked out the window. "She's going to pay for this," she said flatly.

"Look, Gretch. Lori didn't do anything either. If you're going to be mad, be mad at Jeremy. It was his idea."

Gretchen turned to stare at me. "Don't blame him. He's a guy. Guys can't help it when girls prance around in front of them, teasing them."

The conversation was getting crazier by the minute.

"Okay, that comment just set us back about fifty years. People are responsible for their own actions. He can control himself if he wants to. And Lori didn't do anything, I promise. She didn't even know who he was."

"Why are you defending her? You're supposed to be my friend."

This could get sticky. "You are my friend. And so is she."

"Well, Miss Madison. You might not be able to have it both ways." She walked off toward the bank of computers along the wall, leaving me to guess at what might be in store.

*　　*　　*

Gretchen was very quiet at rehearsal. Since Gretchen was never quiet, it worried me. She didn't even talk to

Mai. It meant that Gretchen was planning out her revenge. I tried to keep my thoughts on my dinner with Mark, since those were happier thoughts, but I knew that it wouldn't be much longer before Gretchen forced me to choose. And I didn't know if I had the strength to do it. Since Gretchen had brought me back into the popular crowd, school had become different. People talked to me and included me. I was getting invited to parties, and I had even caught a few freshmen pointing me out as someone important. It felt good. Rehearsals didn't give me a chance to do much, but just being invited was comforting. That would all vaporize if Gretchen turned on me.

Then I remembered something that made my stomach turn. She knew about Lori's secret—that she was an orphan in foster care. It wouldn't matter to Gretchen that the adoption was nearly finalized. And I knew Lori didn't want anyone to know. The whole thing made me want to transfer schools and start over. It was all getting to be too much.

*   *   *

"You ready?" Mark found me in the hallway as I gathered up my backpack and coat. His voice broke through the clouds in my head. *I was going out with Mark!* Well, sort of, anyway. Even if he didn't call it a date, I was still going to be alone with him. I had called my dad at work and asked if I could "grab dinner with some of the cast" tonight. He had said yes, but I still felt guilty that I hadn't been more specific, since his answer probably would have been different. But I didn't feel guilty enough not to go.

"Sure," I said with a smile. "Lead the way."

Since we both had cars, I followed him to The Rock Garden, a small dinerlike restaurant that a bunch of kids usually hung out in. I was surprised he had suggested going there. It was kind of a public place to be, and word would get around that we were there together. I wondered if he realized that. He had only moved to town as a freshman, but surely he knew the gossip that came out of that place. I got more nervous as I drove. Trying to think of intelligent things to talk about was pointless; my mind was mush. I was just hoping I could speak intelligibly by the time we got there.

He came over to my car as I was climbing out. I couldn't help but smile. He didn't say anything until we got settled in a booth toward the back of the restaurant. It would have been nice to sit in the outdoor patio. It was surrounded by a huge garden that you could walk through on a small stone path to look closer at the shrubs, flowers, small trees, and, of course, rocks. It would only be a few more weeks and it would spring into bloom, but right now it still had that frozen winter look. Even though it was cold out, it would be pretty romantic to walk through that garden, with dusk falling and the moon beginning to shine. I tried to push the thought out of my head. *It's not a date. It's not a date.*

"So, what was the head banging about today?" He sat back against the vinyl red cushion, running his fingers through his brownish-blond hair. It was a little longer than usual and wavy on top, and it probably turned really blond during the summer. I didn't want to stare, but I wanted to drink in the reality that he was sitting across from me, completely focused on me.

"Just some drama with Gretchen again." I stirred my straw in my Dr. Pepper, not sure how much he really wanted to know.

"Gretchen." He shook his head. "Drama seems to follow her around. So what happened this time? Somebody look at her funny?"

"No, Jeremy asked Lori out. She wasn't interested, but Gretchen is furious. She's blaming Lori for it instead of Jeremy."

"Why is Gretchen upset at all? Jeremy told me they had broken up."

"It doesn't matter to her. Gretchen couldn't stand Lori from the moment she saw her."

"Actually, you know, Jeremy asked me about Lori last week."

"Did he? What did you tell him?"

"That he should stay away from her. That she wasn't his type. Jeremy likes girls who will . . . well, you know. Lori doesn't seem to be that kind of girl."

"She isn't." I let that thought sink in for a moment, then added, "But before Gretchen just didn't like her, and now she feels justified in going after her."

Mark turned to thank the waitress as she brought our burgers. He bowed his head for a moment but didn't say anything out loud. I bowed my head too, thanking God for the food and for being with Mark. My emotions were too jumbled up to sort them out. What did God really think about it? Was I even supposed to be there?

"You really think Gretchen will do something to her?" Mark asked.

"Yes, but I don't know what. Gretchen can be awfully creative."

"Let's not talk about Gretchen anymore. Tell me something that I don't know about you."

There was plenty to choose from since he hardly knew me at all. I tried to think of something that was interesting yet not too revealing.

"Butterflies," I blurted. "I mean, I raise butterflies."

"What do you mean 'raise them'?" He took a sip of his drink. It was also Dr. Pepper. I wondered if it was his favorite drink too, or if he ordered it because I did. It was nice to think that maybe we had that in common.

"I buy larvae and take care of them until they're butterflies. In the spring and summer I let them go, but the ones I have now, I have to keep indoors."

"You have some at home right now?"

"Yeah, they just emerged. One of them didn't make it, though." The chrysalis had been hanging for weeks, and I knew it had died. Even though it was just a butterfly, I always felt sad when they died. It was like they had almost experienced the greatest transformation of their lives, but they never got there. It just seemed sad.

"What got you into that?" Maybe he was just being polite, but he seemed very interested.

"Remember that semester project we had to do in freshman biology? Well, that's what I chose as my project, and I just kept doing it."

"Interesting hobby."

"What about you?" Even though I hadn't ever really dated, I knew enough to turn the conversation.

"Me? Well, I don't do anything exciting really. Oh, I play the guitar—you probably didn't know that."

"Really? I've always wanted to learn to play an instrument," I gushed. *Relax.* A little less emotion would be good.

"I could teach you," he offered.

"Oh, I don't have one. A guitar, that is."

"Well, if you ever get one, I'd be glad to help you out."

I mentally added a guitar to the very top of my birthday wish list.

Before long we finished up and decided that it was time to head home. As we walked out the door, he put one hand on my back to guide me out. It sent chills down my spine. Such a little thing, but I couldn't help but hope it meant so much more.

I had almost forgotten about the Gretchen-Lori mess until I got home and found a message from Gretchen on the voice mail. It just asked me to call her back, but I knew what it was about. And I didn't want to call her. Not when that warm blanket of happiness from being with Mark was still wrapped around me. But I knew she'd be ticked if I didn't. I couldn't afford to make her any angrier with me. So I called, grudgingly.

"Hey, Gretch. What's up?"

"'Bout time you called. Rehearsal ended two hours ago. Where have you been?"

"Out." I wasn't about to open up my dinner to Gretchen's scrutiny. I'd tell her later when things cooled off.

"Fine, whatever. I just called to tell you I have a plan. And I'm going to need your help," Gretchen informed me.

"A plan? What kind of plan?"

"To put that girl in her place."

"That girl has a name, Gretchen. And I told you already; it's not her fault. Jeremy's an idiot."

"Yeah, well, he's my idiot and she needs to stay away from him. She'll learn who's in charge around here."

"I'm not going to help you hurt her. She's my friend." I tried to sound as confident as I could, but standing up to Gretchen wasn't a comfortable place to be.

She ignored my comment and continued. "I can't tell you anything else right now, but I'll let you know when I need you."

I didn't bother arguing with her and just made an excuse to get off the phone. I had a ton of homework to catch up on, and after getting home so late, I really needed to get started. But my mind kept wandering around, trying to figure out what Gretchen was going to do. She had been so distant and aloof on the phone; I couldn't help but wonder how this was going to change everything again.

*　　*　　*

Things at school were eerily calm the next day. Gretchen seemed like a tiger pacing around in a cage waiting to sink her teeth into someone. And I, of course, knew who that someone was. Lori, however, was blissfully unaware of what was happening. I wanted to tell her, but I couldn't bring myself to do it.

And then there was Mark, who stole into my thoughts during the off moments. I daydreamed about his eyes, his smile, and the very fact that he was interested in me. He had told me on New Year's Eve, in the moonlight no less, that he was attracted to me, but that we could only be friends. I was fine with it at the time, because I knew that I probably should concentrate on my relationship with God. Now I wanted it both ways. I wanted to work on my relationship with God *while* I went out with Mark.

Mark had a secret too. Something that happened that made his parents not trust him. Which was why he wasn't allowed to date. But I didn't know how to classify our dinner together. We may have said it was "just as friends," but it didn't feel that way. My heart had a mind of its own.

Rehearsals were intense, and there was no time to daydream about Mark. I knew my part, but I was still trying to get Gretchen's down. Annie was in so many scenes, and I kept getting confused as to which part I was playing. The one thing I had going for me was that Thompson was being very patient. He seemed to sense that I was working hard and couldn't handle any more pressure from him. When he patted my shoulder after one of the songs and said, "Good job," it flooded me with relief. I didn't want to do any more theater, but I didn't want to mess up the play either.

"Gretchen Stanley!" Thompson's voice boomed from the stage. I was sitting in the auditorium running lines with one of the other orphans. There were several people onstage, including Mark, and Thompson was in the center of it all looking rather angry and red all over. Even his bald head looked sunburned. I couldn't help but stop and watch.

"Where is she!" Thompson demanded. He dropped his clipboard on the stage, the loud clatter echoing through the entire room. Everybody was silent.

"I'll go find her," Michael Goodall said. Michael, who was the student director, took off into the left wing, but no one else moved. Thompson's eyes scanned the room and locked on to mine.

"Madison, get up here and run this scene."

I jumped out of my seat and took my place on the stage as quickly as I could.

"We're not going to sit around and waste time. Take it from Warbucks's line." T moved downstage to watch. The scene was going fine, and then out of the corner of my eye I saw Gretchen standing in the left wing with Michael.

"Stop there." He turned and faced Gretchen. "Go take a seat and don't move."

"This is my scene." Gretchen stepped forward to take my place, and I started to leave until Thompson stopped me.

"Beka, get back in place. Gretchen, you will follow my directions. If I have to send someone to look for you every time I need you, you won't be in this play. Do you hear me? Now sit down!" His voice was raised, but he was still controlled. Gretchen was completely undaunted.

"Give me a break; I was just out back," Gretchen said.

"And we've all been waiting, again, for you. Give me an excuse, Gretchen, and I'll throw you off this cast."

"Are you threatening me? You can't do that," she said.

I couldn't believe it. She was the only person I knew who thought they could talk like that and get away with it. The rest of us watched, holding our breath.

Thompson drew in his breath slowly. He looked like he was trying to calm down, but his words still came out like arrows. "Lose the attitude and sit down, or you can go home and stay home."

"Fine. Whatever," she said as she went and took a seat in the first row. Apparently the lead role was worth losing the argument. She crossed her arms and pouted.

Thompson turned his attention back to those of us onstage. "From Warbucks's line again."

*　　　*　　　*

"I can't believe he said that to me. I might just have to go above his cue-ball head and tell someone who can set him straight. No one talks to me like that," Gretchen said as we walked to the parking lot.

"Gretchen, I wouldn't push it if I were you. It's his play. He can replace you if he wants to."

"Yeah, with you. Please. No offense, Beka, but you've never carried a whole play before. It would be a disaster."

"Well, thanks for the vote of confidence," I muttered.

"How am I supposed to know when I'm needed? I can't just sit around and wait."

"That's what everybody else does, Gretchen. You're the only one nobody can ever find. And you're in practically every scene. Where do you go, anyway?"

"Just around. Why?"

"Gretchen."

"Well, it's really nobody's business."

I rolled my eyes. "Look, I don't care where you've been, but you're pushing it with T."

"T needs to get over himself." She laughed and covered her mouth. "Okay, fine, I'll tell you. I met a guy—totally cute and just dangerous enough to keep things interesting."

"What does that have to do with rehearsals?"

"He doesn't go to school here, so he comes by during rehearsals." She waited for a moment, then continued. "Actually, when I pointed you out to him the other day, he mentioned that he's met you before."

"Really? What's his name?"

"Randy. Randy Yardman."

I shook my head. "I don't know anybody named Randy."

"Well, he knows you." She tilted her head and smiled, but it was a weird smile that made me antsy to get out of there.

"Well, I'll see you tomorrow."

"Keep Wednesday night open. I have an idea," she said as she unlocked her car.

I didn't respond, but she probably just assumed that I would do whatever she asked.

*　　*　　*

I twirled my hair around my finger as my dad and I waited in the small lobby of the counseling center. He had come with me, but I didn't know if that helped me or bothered me. We were the only ones there.

"You feeling okay?" he asked me.

"Sure, why?" I didn't look over at him but kept staring at the ends of my hair. I needed a haircut.

"You just seem quiet tonight," he said.

"I'd like to skip all this." I gestured toward the closed door of the counselor's office. I decided to take a shot. "Really. I'm fine. I don't need to be here. Can we just cancel?"

"No, I've been praying a lot about this. I feel this would be good for you. You still have a hard time talking about what's going on in your life."

"Nothing's going on. This play takes up all my time."

"I would imagine that there are still things happening in your life. I just want to make sure there is somebody who can help you. I know you don't necessarily want to tell me everything that happens at school with your friends, so this is a good alternative."

"That's why I'm here. So that I can talk to some stranger about all the junior class soap operas?"

"No, you're here because you wanted to kill yourself." He choked out the words. "It still worries me that you got to that point."

"I didn't do anything," I protested.

"But you were thinking about it. How can I be sure that you won't start thinking about it again if something happens that makes you feel trapped again?"

I didn't know how to answer that. I was so busy with the play that it offered me an escape from myself. I had purposely put all the events before Christmas out of my head. Before I could come up with an answer, the office door opened.

"See you next week." The counselor waved good-bye to a short man with glasses who nervously waved to her, then to us, then to her again before he pushed open the door. I hadn't known she was a woman. She was tall with her blonde hair cropped stylishly short. She wore heels and a navy pantsuit with a collarless sweater underneath. The fact that she looked so fashionable and relaxed was the only reason I thought I'd give her a shot. I was just glad that she wasn't some stodgy old lady with glasses and frosted hair who wouldn't remember a thing about what it was like to be sixteen. This woman looked like she might.

"Mr. Madison, it's nice to meet you. And you must be Beka. I'm Julie Farnsworth." She shook both of our hands and invited us into the office.

It was a good-sized office with two high-backed leather chairs and a cushy loveseat. I went for the love-seat. My dad and Ms. Farnsworth settled into the other two chairs, and she immediately took charge.

"I invited you both in for this first session so that everyone is on the same page with their expectations. I've talked to your dad on the phone, but I wanted us to talk it over in person. Okay?"

After we both nodded she continued. "Beka, I'm glad you are here today. I know it must feel dreadful coming to a place like this, but I hope you'll find that it's not too bad. Coming here doesn't make you crazy or weird or pathetic."

She read my mind.

She pulled two papers off her desk and handed one to Dad and one to me. She said, "This paper basically explains the confidentiality for minors. Beka, I can promise you that anything you say to me will be confidential unless I specifically tell you that I am going to talk to your father about it. And I would only do that in extreme circumstances. Does that sound all right?"

I nodded and she told my dad to wait in the other room while we got "acquainted" with each other. Once we were alone, she pulled her chair just a little closer and made herself more comfortable in the chair. I felt awkward. Even though she had said being here didn't make me crazy, I sure didn't feel normal.

"So, before we get started, do you have any questions you'd like to ask? You can ask anything at all."

I thought for a moment. "How much does this cost?"

She smiled. "Why?"

"I don't know. I guess it just seems weird to pay somebody to listen to me talk."

"Believe me, we'll do more than just talk. What we'll be doing is real work. It's a different kind of work, but it's work just the same."

"You didn't answer my question."

She smiled again. "It's about eighty dollars an hour.

But your insurance will pick up part of the tab. Anything else?"

"How long do I have to keep coming here?" I was hoping she'd say, "Oh, just a few weeks," and I'd be done. That's not what she said.

"That all depends on you. We'll talk about what we want to accomplish together, and every so often we'll look at how we're doing. I'm not sure what the problems are yet, so it would be hard for me to estimate it right now."

She waited a minute, and when I didn't say anything else, she asked, "Do you mind if I ask you a question?"

"Go ahead." I wished I had brought something to fidget with. I couldn't figure out what to do with my hands.

"You're a junior, right? Tell me about your school."

And so we talked about school. She asked who my friends were, about the subjects I liked, and what special interests I had. I told her about the play and the newspaper and taking pictures, but I made the mistake of adding, "But I don't do anything special."

"What do you mean special?"

"Well, my sister is a gymnast, or she will be again, and my brother plays baseball. Gretchen lives and breathes theater. I just don't do anything interesting."

"It sounds like you do lots of interesting things—the play, the yearbook, the newspaper."

"I do them, but it's not like I would be devastated if I didn't. There's nothing that I love to do."

"What have you tried?"

"Just the things I told you. Not having a 'special' thing never really bothered me before."

"And it bothers you now?"

I nodded and dropped my head. She was easy to talk to, and I was feeling pretty comfortable up until that point. I couldn't articulate what was bothering me, so I felt awkward all over again.

"Well, Beka, I'd like us to talk more about that topic when we get together next time, because we're just about out of time for today. In the meantime, I'd like you to read Psalm 139. Just read it and we'll talk about it next week. Okay?"

I nodded and we went and joined my dad in the waiting room. He didn't ask about what happened. I figured she must have told him not to, because I knew that he was dying to talk to me about it. For once I had a secret I didn't have to feel guilty about.

*   *   *

I was beginning to wonder what Gretchen's master plan was when Friday came and went without so much as a peep from her. She was on her best behavior at rehearsal even though she definitely had an attitude about it. I assumed I'd just have to wait to see what was going to happen.

As I got ready to go to Nancy's on Saturday afternoon, I couldn't help but wonder how I was supposed to handle it when I did find out. No matter what, it was bound to be mean. I hadn't really taken time to pray or do much of anything with God like I said I would. Maybe if I had, I would know what to do. I still had Psalm 32:8 memorized, "I will instruct you and teach you in the way you should go; I will counsel you and watch over you." Did that mean just with spiritual things, or was He interested in all this mess at school too?

Even though I knew that Nancy and her friends would be light-years ahead of me in the God department, I figured it couldn't hurt to sit down and read some of my Bible before I left. Since Julie had given me Psalm 139 to read, I decided to start there.

I read it over and over, letting it sink into my heart. It was the first time I had read Scripture and felt something. I couldn't describe it. It was almost like God was right there with me. "O LORD, you have searched me and you know me. You know when I sit and when I rise; you perceive my thoughts from afar. You discern my going out and my lying down; you are familiar with all my ways. Before a word is on my tongue you know it completely, O LORD."

God knew who I was, even if I didn't. He even knew about little things like when I sit and stand. I remembered Lori's mom had mentioned a verse about God having the very hairs on our head all numbered. If He knew me that well, then He knew about everything that was going on in my life. For the first time since the night I got saved, I felt God's love toward me. And it made me want to love Him back. I just wasn't sure how to do that. How does God want to be loved? I read the psalm again. I was determined to try and know God better. I didn't want to keep putting it off. *Help me know how, Lord. Help me know how.*

I pulled into Nancy's driveway at six on the button. She had called me earlier in the week asking me to come straight to her house for dinner since the concert had been postponed. The concert would have been a nice way to ease myself into the group. Now I didn't have a buffer, and my stomach churned because of it. I didn't see anybody else there yet. I knew I should have tried to get there late. I was always the first one to get anywhere. I sat in my car wondering if I should go in.

A few minutes later I realized that Nancy was standing in her doorway looking out of the storm door. She smiled when she caught my eye. *I should have gone in.* I hadn't even gotten out of my car, and I already felt stupid. I climbed out and Nancy came out onto the porch. To her credit, she didn't mention me sitting in my parked car.

"I'm glad you came, Beka!"

"Thanks for inviting me." I hauled my sleeping bag and backpack up the stairs to the front porch. She gestured toward a rocking chair, so I took a seat and she pulled a white end table over and sat on it.

"I'm just waiting for the pizzas. I hope everyone gets here before they do."

"Who's everyone?"

"Well, you met Allison. Then there's Morgan, Rachel . . ." She ticked each name off on a finger. "And you and me. That's it, five of us. I didn't want to overwhelm you, but I wanted you to get a chance to meet some other girls too."

I shifted in my chair. "So this is all on my account?" *Talk about pressure.*

"Sort of. I mean, we like to get together. It was just a good excuse to do a sleepover."

"Oh." Before I could respond, a car pulled into the driveway, and a girl with a brunette bob jumped out of the passenger side.

"Bye, Mom. See you tomorrow." She opened the rear door and pulled her stuff out of the backseat.

"Hey, Nancy!" she said as she reached the porch. I recognized her from church, but I hadn't really met her.

"Hey, Morgan. This is Beka Madison. She's Paul's sister."

"Oh yeah. Paul." She grinned as she dropped her sleeping bag and overnight bag on the porch and sat on the top step.

"Oh, don't start, Morgan." Nancy shook her head and looked up. "Lord, help her, please!"

"It's too late, Nancy. I know you want us all to deny the fact that we have hormones, but it's too bad." Morgan turned to me and added, "Nancy apparently doesn't have hormones."

"I have hormones, Morgan. I just don't let them fly around like you all do."

"Okay, I'm lost," I said, raising my hand.

"Morgan has a crush on your brother," Nancy told me.

"My brother? Eww." I couldn't imagine someone having a crush on my serious, baseball maniac brother.

"What? He's cute. And it's not a crush. I just happen to think that he'd make someone, like me, a great husband someday," Morgan said.

Another car pulled up and parked behind mine. Allison climbed out of the driver's side and a girl with long dark hair, Rachel, I assumed, got out of the other side. Before they even made it to the porch, the Domino's delivery guy pulled in and carried two large pizza boxes up to the porch. After Nancy paid him she ushered us all into her house and back toward a large family room, complete with a fireplace and a big screen TV.

"Josh! You're not supposed to be down here. Mom said I could have this room tonight," Nancy said as she carried the pizza boxes in and laid them on a coffee table.

"I'm leaving. Don't get all worked up." He tossed one of the pizza boxes open. "But I need some dinner first." He gave her a wide grin and took a slice. He turned and I got my first full view of Nancy's older brother. She had mentioned him before, but she had left out the part about him being the best-looking guy I had ever seen in our small town. Mark was definitely cute, but in a boyish kind of way. Josh was striking and seemed older with his dark eyes and hair. He had the angular build of an athlete, and I found myself imagining him playing soccer or basketball, all out of breath and sweat ringing his hair. A voice jarred me from my thoughts.

"I know you and you and you, but you're a new addition." Josh stood directly in front of me, his eyes sparkling and his hand held out in front of him.

I shook his hand, but I couldn't find my voice.

"That's Beka," Allison said as she pushed past everybody to get into the family room. Morgan and Rachel also went into the room, leaving me standing there, with my hand in Josh's.

"It's Madison, right? Paul's little sister. He's mentioned you before."

That killed my fantasy. I could just imagine what Paul might have said to him. Besides, I already liked Mark. Which is why I couldn't figure out why I felt so drawn to Josh. He obviously didn't feel the same way, because all he said was "Nice to meet you," and he was gone.

Nancy took Rachel with her to get drinks and napkins from the kitchen, and Allison, Morgan, and I sat down on the floor.

"Josh is a hottie, isn't he?" Morgan nudged my arm.

"What? Oh, I don't know." I didn't know her well enough to be honest.

"Yeah, you and every other girl in church, Morgan," Allison said. "You see, Beka, not coming to Sunday school has made you miss out on the Harvest Fellowship matchmaking game. Josh and your brother are absolutely every girl's top picks. They're both smart, athletic, nice, not to mention fine. Yup, they have everybody swooning, but they just smile and keep on walking."

"What she means is that they don't seem interested in the dating scene at all," Morgan explained.

"Paul's always busy with baseball or training or school. He doesn't have much time." I knew I didn't have to defend him, but I felt I should say something.

Nancy and Rachel came back and joined us on the floor.

"So what's the topic?" Nancy asked.

"Boys," Morgan said and then burst out laughing. "What else?"

"We are not going to talk about boys," Nancy insisted. "Let's talk about something else."

"Now wait a minute," Rachel jumped in. She pushed her glasses up on her small nose. "I think it's a good topic—Beka has never been in on our discussions."

Allison leaned over and whispered loudly enough for everyone to hear. "Nancy is our resident pastor. She's always telling us to remember God."

"You make me sound like some killjoy, Allison. I'm not. It's just that it's a delicate area where any one of us could make big mistakes. I just don't like playing around with my heart, because I know it can go one way when God wants me to go the other."

"What do you mean?" I asked. It worried me that my feelings toward Mark could possibly be wrong. I guess, in some way, I assumed that because Mark and I were attracted to each other, it meant that the feelings were okay. Maybe I wasn't supposed to do anything about them yet, but eventually the relationship would work out. But between Josh setting off some brief fireworks in my heart and Nancy's comment, I felt all befuddled, unsure whether I could even trust my own feelings.

"It's just that we can let our emotions get ahead of us sometimes. It makes it harder to hear what God might be trying to tell us."

"You know we love you, Nancy." Morgan pushed her shoulder gently. "We just like giving you a hard time."

"Yeah," Allison added. "We'd all probably be in a mess if it weren't for you reminding us about God. All the time."

The discussion strayed around all different topics as we finished our pizza and then popped a movie in.

Nancy's parents came in and said hello, but we were pretty much left to ourselves. It was all so different than I had thought. I had gotten this idea that they would all sit around quoting Scripture or singing hymns, but they didn't. I did hear them talk about "praying for" and feeling "led" to do lots of things. I wondered what it felt like to have God lead you. Was it a feeling? Or a voice? I longed to know. It would make my life so much easier if God would just tell me what to do. They all seemed to talk about it so naturally too. I hadn't even mentioned God to anyone but my family and Lori, but instead of feeling guilty, I felt strangely motivated.

At one point, the topic drifted to how hard it was sometimes to share Christ with other people. That was when Gretchen's name popped into my thoughts. I pushed it aside but then wondered if maybe that was God trying to speak to me. I couldn't be sure, but I was sure that she would be the hardest person for me to talk about my faith with. Especially since she always made me feel small and crippled for believing, even when I didn't really believe. It did help that I wasn't the only one that had a hard time sharing what I now knew to be the truth.

When we had all gotten ready for bed, we spread the sleeping bags out in a circle with our heads all facing toward the center.

"So what's going on with everybody? Really. How can we pray for each other?" Nancy looked around the circle.

"I'll go first," Morgan volunteered. "I know we joked about it before, but I really have been struggling with my emotions. I get a new crush on a new guy every couple of weeks. And instead of thinking about God, I think about a guy. My heart has a mind of its own."

"Well, I think I need to talk to this girl at my school about God, but I keep chickening out," Allison said.

That one surprised me. Allison didn't seem to be fazed by anything.

"I'm still feeling jealous of Melinda. I don't want to feel this way. I really need God to help me," Rachel added.

"Melinda is her younger sister," Nancy explained. "She has Down's syndrome."

They all looked toward me as if it was my turn.

"Well, I want to spend more time with God." They all murmured that they did too. Then I added, "And I kind of would like to know what that means."

Nancy said, "I really want to know where God wants me to go to school next year. So I'd like you all to pray that God leads me to the school where He wants me. Is that everything? Okay, let's pray."

The next morning was a hustle to get ready in time for church. We had stayed praying and talking well into the night, and I actually enjoyed it. I felt like I belonged even though I was just getting started. Some of them, like Nancy, still seemed light-years away, but listening to them pray helped me to get some ideas on how I could pray.

We were all standing around in the kitchen wolfing down granola bars and orange juice when Josh appeared around the corner.

"Hey, Jelly Bean!" Josh grabbed Nancy's head in a wrestling hold. She struggled to get free, and when she did she popped him on the head.

"Quit calling me that in front of other people, you dork."

Josh looked at me and smiled, "It's her fault, you know. She's the one who likes to stick jelly beans up her nose."

"I was four, Josh. You act like it was yesterday!" She tried to sound mad, but she was smiling.

Without taking his eyes off mine, he said, "I never forget anything. It's a gift."

"Or a curse," Nancy added. She pushed him, causing him to trip toward the hallway. "Come on. We have to go."

We all grabbed the rest of our stuff, and everyone headed out ahead of me as I crouched on the floor and wrestled with the zipper on my backpack. In my rush this morning, I had zipped my pajama top into the zipper, and I couldn't seem to get it free.

"Can I help you with that?" Josh crouched next to me. He didn't say anything, but he smiled when he saw the cherry pattern on the cloth. I was mortified. The damsel in distress routine didn't work well for me—why couldn't it have been something a little less embarrassing?

"There you go." He had the cloth dislodged in about a second.

I tried to say thanks, but I just ended up smiling—a bit too broadly I think. *Great, now I'm a mute damsel in distress.*

He picked up my backpack and sleeping bag and gestured me ahead of him.

"So, I hear you've gotten yourself together now," he said.

I immediately found my voice again. "What are you talking about?" I could feel the panic rising up in my chest. *What does he know?* My mind started whirling with the awful possibilities.

"Don't worry. Paul's not spreading stories or anything. He just mentioned that you had straightened things out with God. I was glad to hear it."

"Oh." What was I supposed to say to that?

We reached the driveway and he put my stuff in the car, as well as Morgan's stuff, because she was riding to church with me.

"God is worth the sacrifice, Beka. I promise." Josh smiled and headed for Nancy's car.

I climbed into the car and only smiled when Morgan grinned, poked me, and pointed toward Josh. *What did he mean by that?* I couldn't even imagine.

*   *   *

Because Gretchen had arranged this Wednesday thing, I went to school Monday morning worried only about a chemistry test that day. Mr. Widman was the only teacher I had who was mean enough to schedule a Monday test. I had spent most of Sunday afternoon studying for it but still felt a little shaky about the material.

So I was surprised when Gretchen slipped me a note during second period.

Beka,
It's already begun☺
Gretchen

The words made my throat tighten. What had begun? She looked back at me, and I lifted my shoulders and hands, silently asking her what she was talking about. She just smiled wickedly.

All my knowledge of chemistry drained out of me as it was replaced by mild panic and whirling thoughts. I noticed my heart beating faster and the air in the room suddenly growing thicker. I put my head down on my desk as my stomach churned. *Oh, Lord, please. I'm not ready for this. Make it all go away.* I thought about that for a few moments. It wasn't going to just go away. So what I really needed was help. I tried again. *Lord, help me through this. Please help me to know what to do.* I didn't get an answer, but my heart slowed down, and I felt a sense of peace. By the time I left second period, I felt ready for whatever was ahead.

But I wasn't ready. Not at all.

*　　*　　*

It wasn't until seventh period that I found out what Gretchen had done. I was typing an article on the computer when Gretchen came over and whispered in my ear, "Check the bulletin board."

So I pulled up the electronic bulletin board on the school's server and found it. Morbid curiosity overtook my common sense, and I read.

Dirty Little Secret
You thought that just because we lived in a small town we weren't at risk for the vile acts committed

at other high schools around this country. But what happens when larger schools send their vermin, the lowest of the low, their most dangerous students away? They could end up at schools like ours, as we walk around, ignorant of the danger that lurks in our midst in a form we would never recognize.

The new girl in town just isn't what she seems, folks. I consider it my public duty to inform you of the risks you incur each day by simply coming to school. She may look innocent, but there's a dirty little secret being hidden from view.

That's all there was. I scrolled down the bulletin board and found that there were dozens of responses to "Dirty Little Secret," mostly wondering what the secret was and guessing who it was about. Many had already guessed correctly. I wondered if Lori had seen it yet.

I looked over at Gretchen, sitting smugly at her desk. She couldn't just kill her victims; she slowly tortured them instead. Even as I sat there, kids in unknown parts of the school were logging in and posting their responses. I logged off and went back to my article, staring at it rather than reading it. What could I do?

*   *   *

At rehearsal, Gretchen grabbed me and pulled me around the corner.

"So?" she asked.

"So what?"

"You can be so frustrating, Beka! What did you think?"

"You're crazy, Gretchen. They're going to catch you. You can get in an awful lot of trouble for posting rumors and gossip on that board. You know that."

"How juvenile do you think I am? I have that covered. I have no less than six different log-on names and passwords, virtually untraceable back to me."

"How did you get those?" It always unnerved me when she got her way no matter what the obstacle.

"Oh, Beka. I have sources everywhere. Don't forget that."

"What's that supposed to mean?" I felt threatened, cornered.

"Just in case you were thinking of protecting that girl." Her words hung in the air for a moment before she changed the subject. "Don't forget about Wednesday. Right after rehearsal."

She didn't give me a chance to respond before she disappeared around the corner. I would just have to wait and see how the saga unfolded and hope that I didn't get caught in the middle.

Lori was waiting for me at my locker the next morning. I could see her from down the hallway as she leaned on the blue metal and looked around. I immediately slowed my pace. If she had seen the posting, I wasn't sure what I was going to say. But even worse was the idea that she hadn't seen it yet. Should I tell her? I owed it to her to warn her, but as long as she didn't know she couldn't get hurt. I wasn't sure which would be worse.

"Hey. How's it going?" I asked when I reached her.

"Pretty good." She grinned. "You'll never believe what happened."

I sighed. Why did our conversations keep starting

like this? I waited for her to tell me while I hung up my coat and got my books.

"Brian called me." She grinned even bigger.

"Brian? The guy from the New Year's Eve party?" It was bizarre that we had just talked about him and now he was calling her.

"Yeah. I'm not even sure how he got my number. But he called and asked me to go to a dance. He's home-schooled and I guess all the home-schooled kids have this formal dance, and he called and asked me to go. Can you believe it?"

"That's great. Are David and Megan cool with it?" They were only a week away from officially being her parents, but I didn't know if I should call them her "mom and dad" yet or not.

"Totally. Megan knows his mom from the studio, so she was fine with it. I'll have a curfew and everything, but they're going to buy me a dress . . ." Her eyes teared up and she looked away for a minute.

"What's wrong?" I stopped moving and turned toward her.

She looked back and smiled through her tears. "Nothing. Nothing at all. I'm just happy. For the first time in my life I feel like a normal kid. It just over-whelms me sometimes." She got ahold of herself and said that she'd tell me more at lunch, and then she ran off to class.

I really was happy for her, but I couldn't ignore a small stab of jealousy in my gut. Here Lori was, not only getting a new family but going out with this great guy she just met. Why couldn't my life be normal too? Why couldn't Mark take me out on a legitimate date? I felt cheated. It figured that the guy I happened to like was technically unavailable—and I still didn't even know why.

*   *   *

Another note landed on my desk during English.

Beka,
Don't forget to check the board. I'm sure
you'll find it fascinating☺
Gretchen

I wouldn't have a chance to check it before journalism, but maybe that was for the best. I could talk to Lori at lunch without knowing the full scope of what Gretchen might have written.

*   *   *

"So, he just called you out of the blue?" I asked as we settled down at our table.

"Yeah. I haven't seen him since the party. He actually apologized for not calling me sooner."

"So? Details, please."

"Well, I already told you he's home-schooled and that our moms know each other. I just was so surprised he asked me. I mean, we only met that one night. I thought he was really cute and sweet and nice, but I didn't know that he had really noticed me. But he did! I'm so excited."

"Well, you must have made an impression." How

could she not make an impression? She was beautiful, smart, and knew how to dress. There was that jealousy pang again.

"I guess. You know, he's been home-schooled all his life. He's never been to a real school. And he's from a big family too. He's the oldest, and he's got two brothers and three sisters." Lori shook her head. "I can't imagine living in a house with that many people."

"So this dance will be all home-schooled kids."

"Mostly. They can ask anyone they want, but they have this group of families that all home-school, and they do this formal dance once a year so the kids don't miss out on stuff like that. Brian said that he doesn't know how to dance real well, but I don't care. It'll be fun to get dressed up and go out like that."

"You could ask him to come with you to the junior prom, you know."

"That's not till May, right? I guess I should wait to see how his dance goes first. I told him about me dancing at church, and he thought that was really cool. He might even come to the dance concert when we do it."

"What dance concert?"

"The teacher, Miss Haverty, is putting together a dance concert this spring. The date's not set yet, and I'm not even sure I'll be in it. I just started classes, but she said I might be able to be in a couple of the dances anyway."

I got the feeling that Lori was being modest.

"Will you come to the dance concert if I can be in it?" she asked.

"Sure. It sounds interesting."

"I'd still like you to take classes with me. I think you'd like it."

I shook my head. "Not me. I've been trying to think of something to get involved with. But I haven't been hit with any brilliant ideas yet."

"Megan said that she'd work with you at her photography studio, remember? You could do that."

"Maybe. I love photography and all, but I don't know. Do you really think she meant it when she offered?"

"Absolutely. You should do it. And if you don't like it as much as you thought, there's no harm done. Right?"

"True. But it will have to be after this play is finished. My whole life is on hold, it feels like."

"But Mark's in the play. You get to see him every day."

"Sort of. We aren't in a lot of scenes together, but I do see him. Actually, we had dinner last week. That was nice."

"Nice! Why didn't you tell me you had a date with him?"

"It wasn't a date. It was a . . . dinner. Just two friends having dinner."

"Friends? You go out on a date, but it's not a date. What does that mean?"

"I don't know," I admitted. I glanced at my watch and realized we only had a minute or so. Either I said something about the posting now, or I was going to lose my chance to warn her.

"Do you use the computers at school much?" I blurted out.

"Huh? Talk about subject swap. Um, no, not really. I think I'm going to have to learn to use the server for yearbook, but I don't start that until next week, and I've kind of missed most of the year as it is. Why?"

"Oh, it's nothing. We better go so we're not late for fifth. See ya later."

She said good-bye and we went in opposite directions. Well, she wouldn't see it firsthand, but I knew it would get back to her sooner or later.

*　　*　　*

When it was finally work time in journalism, I went straight to the computers. I had to read it simply so I would know what I was up against. I logged on to the server and pulled up the bulletin board. The first section had been removed, along with a lot of the responses, and in its place was a warning.

This bulletin board was designed for the purpose of letting our students know about activities and events that might be of interest to them. It was NOT designed to transmit gossip or rumors of any sort. Those that are responsible for yesterday's posting are hereby warned not to post anything of this sort again. This will be your only warning, and if it happens again, the appropriate action will be taken.

Ouch! That ought to put a stop to this, I thought. I glanced around to see where Gretchen was. She was hunched over her desk writing furiously. I logged off the computer and went back to one of the worktables to finish up the story I was working on.

I had just begun to relax and focus on the story when Gretchen came up behind me and cleared her throat.

"Can I help you?" I asked.

"I need to talk to you." She led me to a couple of desks that were away from where the rest of the class was, and we sat down.

"Can you believe that message on the computer?" she started.

"Yes. Gretchen, please. You knew it was risky." I wanted to add that she was posting a pack of lies but figured it wouldn't go over very well.

She drummed her fingers on the table, her face hard. "Well, it's not over till I say it's over. I'm going to re-post it right before school tomorrow." She shoved a paper in front of me. "Want a sneak preview?"

"No." I pushed the paper back at her.

"Aw, come on! The whole school is dying to hear the rest of the story. And you get to be first. You should be honored."

"Honored?" I didn't say anything else, but I did take the paper and read it. My curiosity got the better of me. There were two separate parts to the story.

The Dirty Little Secret
Part II

Even though some people in our administration want to protect you from the knowledge of this secret, I want each of you to stay informed about what's really going on at our school. The girl I referenced in the earlier section is truly the worst kind of student to have in our halls. One that looks innocent. One that looks safe. One that looks harmless. But she is in fact none of the above. She came to our school with a sordid past. One that could put our boys in danger and our girls at risk. The truth I will reveal to you is shocking, I know. I could hardly believe it myself. And at first, you won't want to believe it could be true. You won't be able to imagine that such an innocent-looking girl could be involved with such horrible things. But you must believe it. For your own safety and the safety of the school.

The Dirty Little Secret
Revealed

The time has come to reveal the truth, now that you all are ready to hear it. The girl who I've been telling you about, the one hiding among us like a cheetah watching for prey, is LT. I can only give you her initials, but you will know who I am speaking of. She came to this school because she was kicked out of her previous one. For what, you ask? One word—drugs. But the drugs were only a part of it. Just a tip of the iceberg. Because she wanted her drugs, it led her into the dark underworld of weapons and prostitution. That can't be! you might say. But it's true. She was willing to risk anybody's safety for her own satisfaction. Including her own father's. Do we want a girl roaming the halls that could turn on us? One that could put our very lives in danger? And I have only told you part of the story . . .

I couldn't even speak. I looked at Gretchen and just

shook my head until I could get my brain and tongue to work together.

"This is outrageous, Gretchen. Not to mention completely ridiculous."

"I'm going to post one tomorrow and the other one on Friday. The powers-that-be are waiting to strip it, so I'll probably have to post it a couple of times for maximum exposure."

"Are you listening to me? These are lies, Gretchen, completely crazy lies. No one is going to believe you."

She turned and looked at me. "It's true, Beka. It's true if I say it's true. No one will go near her."

"Gretchen. Listen to me. Think about what you're doing. You could get in a lot of trouble for this. This is slander. It could ruin an innocent person's reputation."

"Innocent?" her voice went up.

"Okay, it's clear you don't care about her. But think about yourself. This could go on your record. Colleges could see it. You're going to throw away your future over some petty little incident."

"They're not going to catch me. I told you. They can't trace it back to me. And don't even think about tipping them off, Beka, or it will come threefold back on you." She stood up and smiled that wicked smile. "Don't forget about tomorrow." She walked away.

I looked down at the paper still in my hands. It was written freehand, but it wasn't in Gretchen's handwriting. I wondered for a moment if maybe Mai had written it.

"Beka," Ms. Adams's voice came from behind me. I folded the paper quickly and shoved it in my notebook so she wouldn't see it.

She held out a folder to me. "Could you proofread this story for me before you go today?"

"Sure." I smiled and took the folder.

"I'm looking forward to seeing you in the play, Beka," she said.

"Thanks. I hope it goes okay. I'm kind of nervous about it."

"Oh, while I have you here, let me ask you a question. I've been thinking about who to appoint as editor next year, and since you'll be a senior I wondered if you wanted to have some input. I'm going to talk to all the seniors before I decide. So, who do you think would be a good editor?"

"I don't know." It was my big chance to talk to her about it, and I was going to blow it if I didn't speak up.

"You must have some thoughts about it. You've been with me since you were a freshman."

"I guess Olive would be good at it." *You're blowing it! Speak up!*

"Olive does have a knack for writing, but I'm also concerned about people skills. I want somebody who can give the paper direction but at the same time encourage the other students toward a . . . a higher level of responsibility. Who do you think would be able to do that?"

"I don't know." *What is wrong with you!*

"What about you? Would you be interested in being editor?"

"Me?" I took a deep breath. Okay, the conversation was started, and now all I had to do was keep it going. She was waiting.

"I guess I have thought about it. But I don't really

know if I'd be good at it or not. I've never done anything like that before."

"That's what school is all about, Beka. Trying new things, flexing your wings, and finding out what you're good at. I think you'd do a good job as editor. It would stretch you, I think, but in a good way. I know this last year has been tough on you, but the editor job doesn't start until the fall. Do you think you'd be up to it?"

"If you think I'd be able to do it, then I'd be up for trying."

"That's all I needed to know. I still need to talk to some other students before I make my final decision. I'll let you know as soon as I can. Sound good?"

"Sure. Thanks, Ms. Adams." I couldn't help but smile.

I got to school extra early that morning so that I could go to the computer lab and see if Gretchen was going to risk posting her lies. Mrs. Palmer was just opening up the lab when I got there.

"I have to run and make some copies. But you can go on in if you want and turn them on." Mrs. Palmer disappeared down the hallway, limping slightly on her artificial leg.

I went in, turned on one of the computer banks, and waited for them to boot up. When they did, I logged on and pulled up the bulletin board.

It was one of the top postings. I scanned it quickly to see if it was what Gretchen showed me yesterday. She only posted the first of the two new stories, once again dragging out the torture. I figured it wouldn't be up for long before one of the teachers found it and stripped it off. Several other kids came into the lab, whispering about the post. They were obviously looking for the next installment. My stomach turned as I logged off and headed for homeroom. I was going to have to say something to Lori. Today.

*   *   *

I was working up my nerve to tell her while we were in the lunch line. But when we sat down, she beat me to it.

"Have you seen this?" She handed me a piece of paper. It had the first and second posts printed out on it. I felt like throwing up.

"Yes," I admitted. I would completely understand if she was mad at me for not telling her.

But instead of getting upset, she laughed.

"Isn't that ridiculous?"

"Yes, it's completely ridiculous, but . . ."

"But, what?"

"It doesn't bother you? If it were me, I'd be . . . I don't know, upset, mad, both."

"It's all lies. Of course it bothers me, but I know it'll all blow over. These things always do. Before I got pulled out of my house, kids were whispering and spreading rumors about me at my old school. Everything from saying it was my mom's fault that my dad died in that accident to saying that I was doing drugs with my mom. The truth just wasn't as exciting, I guess. And in the long run, it doesn't matter 'cause it's not true. My real friends will know that."

"Lori, you amaze me. There's not even a little part of you that's mad?"

"A little," she admitted. "But I've been reading about how Jesus was treated, and you know, they spread lies about Him too. So it helps that I'm in good company. And it helps that He knows the truth too."

I suddenly felt very guilty. When was the last time I read my Bible? It wasn't ever going to help me if I didn't start reading it. I sighed. It was frustrating to feel like I didn't have any time.

"One thing that does bother me is that I don't know what I did to make someone this mad at me. To go to so much trouble? I can't imagine what I did."

I shrugged. "Who knows." I knew. And I wished that I didn't.

*　　*　　*

After rehearsal, Gretchen, Mai, and Liz were waiting in the hallway for me while I gathered up my things. Gretchen told us we had to move our cars out of the parking lot to the side street so no one would know we were there. I should have known right then that I should just go straight home. But I moved my car with everybody else and walked with them to the football field. Both Gretchen and Mai were carrying duffel bags, and Liz and I exchanged several worried glances.

Gretchen was headed toward the concession stand, or

The Snack Shack as we called it. I thought about making some excuse and turning back, but I couldn't seem to form the thought into words. It was partly curiosity, but it also made me feel special to be included. Gretchen, after all, was one of the most popular girls in school. Most of the girls looked to her for the fashion trends, and if Gretchen dated a guy, any guy, he could go from geek to A-lister overnight. But I never really understood why. Gretchen was cute, but there didn't seem to be anything particularly special about her that made other kids follow her. Maybe if I could figure out what it was, I could quit being one of the followers.

"I thought this would be the best place to meet. Since we don't want any parents or sibs nosing into our business." Gretchen unlocked the rear door to The Snack Shack and flipped a light switch on. The concession windows were shut tight, and the different machines—the hot dog warmer, the popcorn maker, and the cotton candy dispenser—all sat clean and shiny, ready for the next soccer game. Candy and other snacks were stacked three shelves high along the back wall. The smell of popcorn and hot dogs seemed to be imbedded in the thin wood walls. It made me hungry for dinner.

Gretchen pulled a thin blanket from the duffel bag and spread it on the concrete floor, gesturing to all of us to sit down. And, like sheep, we obeyed.

"Tonight, we need to make a pact, and to seal it, we will perform this spell." She held open a book, a thick paperback that looked brand-new.

"Where'd you get that?" Mai asked.

"I ordered it online. And they don't just have spell

books; you can get crystals and all sorts of other stuff. I ordered these for us too." She pulled a small black velvet pouch out of the duffel and spilled the contents into her lap. She untangled four rope necklaces, each with a crystal set in silver dangling in the center. She handed one to each of us. Mine looked like pink marble. It was actually rather pretty. The silver wrapped around the crystal like ivy, and the black cord felt like satin.

"We will wear these to signify our sisterhood. Go on, put them on," Gretchen said.

Mai slipped hers over her head. Hers was a deep blue with white streaks through it, Gretchen's was black, and Liz's was the color of green jade. Liz stared at hers for a moment and I thought for a minute that she would bail me out, but eventually she shrugged and slipped it over her head. That left me staring at the crystal in my palm.

"What's the problem, Madison?" Gretchen was getting impatient.

"Well, I'd like to know what this all is supposed to mean. Sisterhood? Pacts? What are you trying to do?"

"I just felt like we should make a commitment to one another. It's just a loyalty thing; you don't have to get uptight about it. And you don't have to stay either. There's the door." Her voice was sharp, and I knew I was treading a very thin line.

But I kept going. "I doubt that's all there is to it, Gretch."

She stared at me for a moment, and then a smile began to play around the edges of her mouth. "Well, I always said you should get a spine. I just wasn't expecting you to get one with me." She smiled and leaned forward into the circle we had made with our bodies.

"Okay, I'll just tell you since I know that I can trust you guys." When she said that, she looked at each of us as if she was making sure she could.

"I've been doing lots of research about Wicca, and I'm telling you it's just awesome. It's basically up to you to pick and choose what you want to do and what you don't want to do. There's a code that you're expected to follow, but it's stuff you would do anyway. So I thought we should form a sisterhood and vow to be loyal to each other. It'll be fun. We'll get to create our own religion."

"Gretchen, you can't just invent a religion. What about God?" I asked.

"What about Him? See, what's great about this is that you can worship whatever you want. You can worship God and I can worship . . . I don't know, the goddess Diana if I want. I'm not saying that's what I'm gonna do, but I could."

"But there's only one God, Gretchen, if . . ."

"That's where you're being narrow-minded, Madison." Gretchen's voice had taken that edgy tone again. "You can't think that your religion is all there is, or that your God is all there is. Anyway, how do you know that everyone's not praying to the same God and just calling Him different names?"

I didn't know how to answer that, and the conversation was making my stomach hurt. I knew what she was saying wasn't right. I could feel it was wrong, but I didn't know how to explain myself or even make an argument.

When I didn't say anything else, she took her book back into her lap.

"Let's move on. We'll do the pact thing next week. Let's just take this spell and try it together. You'll see, Beka. When this thing works you'll know what I'm saying is true."

She took out some candles and incense from the bag Mai was carrying and then took several minutes to set them up. While she was doing that the rest of us were supposed to be "centering ourselves," whatever that meant. I prayed. Desperately.

Lord, I'm not sure how I got into all this. Help me know what to do. What to say. And please protect me, Lord. I don't want to do anything against You. Help me, please.

I sat there while Gretchen did the spell. Every nerve inside of me was telling me to get up and get out of there, but I couldn't do it. I wasn't ready to face the consequences of defying Gretchen yet. It was kind of a corny spell about protection and power. I didn't really understand what she was trying to do. And I don't think Mai and Liz did either.

When we were walking back to the cars, she said, "We'll meet next week, same time, same place. And remember, you can't tell anybody. I'll know if you do."

I knew that she wouldn't know, but she sounded so sure of herself I nearly believed her. I had tucked the crystal into my pocket, and when I was sitting at the Dairy Queen traffic light, I pulled it out and looked at it. It seemed like just an innocent necklace. Something you'd buy at the beach. But knowing where Gretchen got it and how important the necklaces were to her, I figured it couldn't just be an innocent necklace. I opened up the ashtray, which I only used to throw spare change into, and slipped it inside.

Out of sight, out of mind.

*　　*　　*

I had been in the same homeroom with Mrs. Lauden for three years. And for three years I sat next to Amy Marks simply because of alphabetical order. We politely nodded at each other, but I couldn't remember ever having an actual conversation with her. She seemed nice, but she was one of those superathlete types who played sports all year long: field hockey in the fall, basketball all winter, soccer in the spring, and swimming all summer. Her hair was cropped short, and she always seemed tanned and muscular. We never had anything to talk about. Until today.

"Hey, did you hear what happened this morning?" Amy had scooted her chair a little closer to mine.

I thought she was probably talking about some soccer game, so I just shrugged.

"They caught the person who was writing those posts. She's in the office already. I heard she might be suspended," she said.

I couldn't speak. I was as elated as I was terrified. Someone had actually caught Gretchen. I couldn't believe it.

"Did you hear anything else?" I asked.

"No, except that she's scared to death and denying it all. I never knew she had it in her. She seems so mousy."

I was about to ask what she was talking about, since

"mousy" was about the last word I would use to describe Gretchen, but Mrs. Lauden shushed us and began taking roll.

I heard a couple other people say she was caught, but I didn't hear any new info. I was beginning to feel rather vindicated. Gretchen, Miss Invincible, had been nabbed. But then I got to second period.

And there was Gretchen, sitting smugly in her chair, notebook open and a smile on her face.

"But . . . I thought . . ."

"Quit stuttering, Beka. You sound like a dork," she said.

I took a deep breath and slid into my seat. I didn't know what to say.

Gretchen turned around in her chair and leaned toward me. "Can you believe who was posting those horrible things?" she asked.

I just stared at her. She seemed to be enjoying herself entirely too much.

"Yeah," she continued. "Olive just doesn't seem the type, does she?"

"Olive? Olive! Gretchen, you didn't."

"Shut up, Beka. Keep your voice down."

"You framed Olive? Of all people? She'll deny it, and no one will believe she did it."

"I don't know. The evidence is there. She posted it." Gretchen grinned. "I guess the end will have to wait a few days."

"What?" I was mad. Of all the people she could have hurt, she chose Olive. Meek, mousy Olive. The poor thing was probably terrified.

"Yeah, I suppose things will have to die down before the final chapter is posted." She turned back around in her seat so that she could look like Miss Perfect Student. I scribbled in my notebook, drawing circles harder and harder into the paper. What was I going to do? I stared at the back of Gretchen's curly red head. *Evil, thy name is Gretchen.*

During a break at rehearsal that afternoon, I tried to find a quiet spot to just sit and think. My head was whirling. Olive had not gotten suspended but was on a kind of probation. They apparently believed that perhaps she wasn't to blame, and since they didn't have any other proof, they let her off the hook as long as nothing else happened.

I wondered how long Gretchen was going to wait before she dared to post the last installment. She hadn't said anything during journalism, and I couldn't help but hope that maybe she would reconsider the entire thing.

"What's wrong?"

Before I even looked up, I knew it was Mark. The

warmth of his voice spread through me like hot chocolate on a snowy day.

He sat down beside me and leaned on the concrete wall. I didn't even know where to start. I leaned my head back against the wall and closed my eyes. I was afraid that if I tried to speak I was going to start crying. And that was the last thing I wanted to do.

He waited for a few minutes, but when I didn't say anything he spoke again.

"Let's get out of here." He stood up and held out his hand.

"Rehearsal's going to start again in like—" I glanced at my watch—"five minutes."

He disappeared down the hallway. I wasn't sure if I should follow him, but just when I was about to go after him he reappeared.

"Let's go." He held out his hand again.

"But . . ."

"It's all taken care of."

"Taken care of? We have scenes coming up."

"T said we can go. Promise."

"You asked him?"

He reached down for my hand and pulled me off the floor. And without letting go he walked me back to the band room where thirty-some backpacks were strewn across the floor.

"Get your stuff and let's get out of here." He smiled. "Go on. It's fine."

And so I did. I gathered up my backpack, found my jacket, and followed him out of the school. He opened the front door of his black Celica, and I sank into the seat. He climbed in beside me, revved the engine, and tore out of the parking lot.

The day had just a hint of spring in it, and I opened my window, letting the cool air swirl through my hair and my mind, letting it blow away the worry and the questions that had taken up residence in my thoughts.

He drove and drove. We left town and sped along the back roads, past sleeping cornfields and thick forests. As we drove, the rolling hills gave way to the steeper roads leading into the mountains. I didn't think about where we were going or even if I should be going. I just let the wind blow on my face. And I let him slip his hand into mine.

He didn't say anything until he pulled into a small parking lot surrounded by trees and a brown split rail fence. He climbed out of the car and then came around and opened my door.

"I want to show you something. Follow me."

And I gladly did. He walked toward a break in the fence. It was a trailhead with a brown plaque naming it White Tail Trail. I wasn't dressed for a hike. Even though I was wearing laced shoes, they were high and kind of clunky to be navigating a dirt trail sprinkled with rocks and roots. I didn't ask where we were going. Every once in a while he reached back to help me up a rock, and he tried his best to keep the branches out of my face, but they still pulled at my hair, which was already a mess from letting it fly around in the car. I wished I had brought a scrunchie to pull it back out of my face.

"It's just a little farther, I promise." A few turns of the trail later, he pulled back some branches and we stepped out onto a rock ledge overlooking a waterfall and a large pool of water. The water from the pool made its way into a stream that disappeared off to the right. The trees had not even begun to bud, but even with all the brown branches, it was a breathtaking place. I sat down on the rock and stared at the water. The sound of the water falling was all I could hear. I closed my eyes, listening.

"Isn't it beautiful?" Mark's voice shook me out of my reverie.

I smiled in agreement. "Thanks for bringing me here." I took in a deep breath. "It's so clean and fresh here."

"I actually come out here sometimes. Just to think. Later in the season, this trail will be packed with people, but now . . . now it's all ours." He wrapped both hands around a limb just above his head, swinging slightly against it.

"What do you think about?" I wrapped my arms around my legs, feeling chilled only on the outside.

He thought for a moment before he answered. "My life, I guess. And what a mess I've made of things."

"Your life doesn't seem like a mess." His life seemed pretty charmed to me.

"Looks can be deceiving." He didn't say anything else for several more minutes. He walked over and sat down beside me. "I've made some pretty big mistakes."

"So you mentioned." I wanted to ask, but I held my tongue.

"Her name was Chelsea," he started.

I didn't react on the outside, but on the inside I cringed. I didn't want to hear about some girl! He'd probably tell me she was the love of his life and how he lost her, boo-hoo.

"I went to this camp last summer. It was like this endurance, adventure-type camp, and I was there almost six weeks. My parents were traveling, so I got stuck going. I was mad about it at first but I liked it. Then I met Chelsea. We started hanging out as much as we could, but since we didn't get much time, we started sneaking around to see each other."

I wanted him to stop talking. *Talk about the waterfall. The rabbits. Anything but another girl.*

"She was beautiful. Actually," he said as he turned toward me, "she looked a lot like you."

I wasn't sure whether I should be flattered or frustrated.

He continued. "Anyway. It was a long summer, and near the end we started, well, fooling around more and more. You can probably guess what happened."

I don't want to guess. I want this conversation to stop.

"I didn't find out until school started that she was pregnant."

That nice, clear, warm feeling was now gone, and my thoughts were a whirlwind again. *He had been with someone?* I wasn't naive enough to think that it didn't happen at our age. There were plenty of girls who claimed to be having sex, and more than a few that probably really were. But Mark? I always thought he was different. That he wouldn't do something like that.

"But I thought you were a Christian, Mark. I don't understand . . ."

"I am. And so is she."

"But . . ."

"Everyone makes mistakes, Beka." He sounded defensive.

"I didn't mean . . . It just surprises me, that's all." And it made me uncomfortable. Here I was in this isolated place alone with him having this personal conversation. What felt so good just moments ago now felt all wrong.

"Well, obviously my parents found out when her parents called. They had all these meetings about what to do about the baby and all this stuff. My parents were pretty angry about the whole thing. Which is why I had to agree to the 'no dating' thing. They were even going to pull me out of school and make me go to the Christian Academy, but they backed down about that one."

"So what happened? I mean, are you going to become a father?"

He shuddered. "No, she lost the baby a few weeks later. So it was a moot point."

"Oh my goodness. Is she okay?" My heart immediately turned toward this faceless girl. I felt so bad for her. To have that kind of summer, then come home only to find out she was pregnant and then lose the baby. It must have been awful for her.

"Yeah. She's fine." His eyes took on a faraway look.

"Did you love her?" The words came out before I could stop them. I needed to know.

"I thought I did. But I don't think I really know what that is." He turned and looked at me for a moment and then reached over and brushed some hair away from my eye.

I stood up, ruining the moment. "I think we better get back. My dad will be expecting me home soon."

"You're right." He stood up too. I turned to go, but he grabbed my hand and pulled me back, then he moved his hands to my waist. He was so close I could smell the peppermint on his breath.

"Don't hate me."

"Hate you? Why would I hate you?" I tried to leave again, but he held me firm.

"I didn't have to be honest with you, but I thought you deserved to know."

"Okay." I didn't know what he wanted me to say.

"You're not okay. You all of a sudden want to leave. You're upset with me."

"No. It's just getting late. And dark. I think we should go."

"I don't want to lose you over this. I need to know that you . . . that you're okay."

"I'm fine. Really."

"Prove it to me." He pulled me close to him, turned his head, and kissed me. At first I didn't know what he was doing, and by the time I realized it, his lips were already on mine. For a moment, I let him, but then I pulled away.

"Mark, we shouldn't . . ."

"Why?"

"I thought we were going to be friends." I moved his hands off of me and took a step back.

"Beka, don't be naive. You know I like you."

"I think we should go. Really. It's getting late." I ducked under the tree branch he had swung on and headed down the trail. He didn't answer, but I heard him snapping sticks, following along behind me. He didn't say anything else as we stumbled our way back down the trail. It was harder to navigate the path, and I wished I wasn't leading the way. But I wasn't about to stop. Once we climbed in the car, I opened the window again, hoping the wind would blow away my thoughts on the drive home.

But instead, I thought about everything he had said, turning the conversation over and over in my mind. I couldn't place what he had said that bothered me so much. I knew that people made mistakes. I understood that. But there was something in what he didn't say that moved around in my thoughts. Just knowing the truth had changed my heart toward him. Was I being judgmental? God would forgive him. I knew that—I depended on that forgiveness myself. But I wondered if his heart toward me would change if he knew my weaknesses, my secrets.

He just said good-bye when he dropped me off in the school parking lot. He looked defeated, but I didn't know how to console him without giving him the wrong idea. And even though I had kind of rejected him on that ledge, my heart still ached when he pulled away. I was going to have to figure out what to do pretty quickly, or I was going to lose him. I knew it.

*　　　*　　　*

When I got home there were messages from Gretchen and Lori on the voice mail. I knew I wasn't going to be able to concentrate on my homework until I talked to someone. Only Lori would understand, so I dialed her number first.

"It just bothers me," I told her after I had filled her in on the afternoon.

"I don't blame you. I mean, is that the kind of guy you want to be with? One that would sleep with a girl and then abandon her?"

"He didn't abandon her per se. I don't even think she lives around here."

"It doesn't matter. He didn't really stick with her. I don't know, Beka. It all sounds like a pretty big red flag to me."

"Yeah, it bothers me. But maybe he's learned from his mistake."

"Look, I don't want to sound like a parent about all this, but it sounds to me like he's trying to date you without officially dating you. It's kind of sneaking around, isn't it?" Lori asked.

"Kind of." I blew out a frustrated sigh.

"Subject swap. Can you come over for dinner tomorrow night?"

"I guess so. I have something until six, but after that I'm okay. Why?"

"It's official. As of today I am officially a member of the Rollins family."

"So the adoption went through? That's great." I was sincerely happy for her. And I only had slight twinges of panic as my mind fluttered to Gretchen.

"Yeah. It's kind of been frustrating with the courts and all. We got delayed a couple of times, but everything was signed and sealed today. I've even filed to get my name changed. It's time to leave the past in the past."

We talked for a bit longer, but the conversation never returned to Mark. But I couldn't get my mind off of him. I did feel like I was being deceitful, because Dad had said I could date but that he wanted to get to know the guy. We were seeing each other, but technically they weren't "dates." Even though my dad had actually met Mark the night Mark gave me a ride to his house, my dad would probably want to have him over for dinner or some totally humiliating thing like that. I didn't want to go there if I didn't have to, and I knew Dad would insist on it if he knew.

I hated secrets.

"**So how have** things been going this week?" Julie asked as soon as we got settled in our seats. I had opted for the love seat again, tucking myself into the corner. I had remembered to wear a beaded bracelet this time, and I immediately started sliding the beads around the cord.

"Busy." Dad had let me drive myself to the appointment, and I got there ten minutes too early. I had been fine about coming until I was sitting in the waiting room. It had gotten me all nervous and fluttery inside.

"What's been keeping you busy then?" Even though she was relaxed back in her chair, she seemed to be listening with her whole body.

"School, the play." I shrugged. "No time for much else."

"Working on the play must be fun."

"Yeah, it's all right."

"Why just 'all right'?" she pressed.

I didn't know whether to just blurt it all out or sidestep the question. I was afraid that if I started talking I wouldn't be able to shut up. I glanced at the huge clock on the back wall. We had only been in there five minutes. It was going to be a long hour if I didn't say anything.

So I spilled it. All about trying out for the play even though I hadn't ever done one, how I got a part, and about understudying Gretchen. I also talked about how important Gretchen was at school and how things were better now that she didn't hate me. Julie nodded and said "uhh-hmm" a lot.

When I finished she asked, "Do you always do what Gretchen tells you to do?"

"No." *Liar.* "I don't know. Gretchen is very . . . influential."

"Why do you suppose that's true?"

I thought about that. I didn't know. I couldn't even say exactly when it was that she became popular. Maybe sometime during middle school. She was just a normal girl for a long time, and then somehow, someway, she became an uber-girl.

Julie was patiently waiting for an answer. I started sliding the beads in the other direction.

"Maybe it's . . . well, Gretchen just has a way of making you believe that she's right and everyone else is clueless."

"Do you think you're clueless?"

"No. But I guess I act like I am."

"Why?"

"It's easier. It's easier than fighting the order of the universe. I'm just not important enough." *Wow. Do I really think that?* I hadn't even thought that over before it came out of my mouth.

"Who says you're not important?" Julie was now leaning forward, resting her elbow on her knee and her chin in her hand.

"Everybody, I guess. I just exist."

"What does God say about you?"

I knew that the psalm I read said that I was "fearfully and wonderfully made," but I didn't know what that meant. And I knew the Bible said that thing about all my hairs being numbered, but that seemed a little bizarre to me. I didn't know what to say.

Julie waited for a bit, then said, "Maybe that's where you need to start." She stood up and walked over to her desk, retrieving a piece of paper. "These are some Scriptures I'd like you to look up over the next week. It will give you a sense of how God feels about you."

I took the paper she offered, and she sat back down.

"But I'll tell you something. They will mean very little to you right now."

"Why?" She had my attention now.

"Because right now, even though you believe in God, you don't trust Him enough to believe what He says about you. Yet. But you will. God has a way of helping each of us learn to trust Him and discover how faithful He really is."

*　　*　　*

Driving over to Lori's I turned the music off and just tried to listen. When I told Julie that I didn't always know what to say when I prayed, she suggested that I spend time listening. I wasn't exactly sure what I was supposed to be listening for. A voice maybe? A feeling? I certainly didn't hear anything, but as I pulled into Lori's driveway I realized that I felt okay. I didn't feel panicked or worried. I just felt calm. And with all the things going on, I figured that had to have come from God.

*　　*　　*

Lori's house was packed when I went inside. Her "new" grandparents were there, as well as an aunt and her family. I was the only friend that Lori had invited. I felt honored, especially since I knew she was spending time with some new friends at church.

I never really got a chance to talk to Lori because of all the activity, but right before dinner Megan caught me in the hallway.

"I'm so glad you could join us, Beka!" she said.

"Thanks for having me." I shifted my weight to my other leg.

She leaned against the wall and looked like she was trying to compose herself. Her soft, wavy brown hair fell forward for a moment, and then she lifted her head to look at me. "I wanted to tell you I appreciate all you've done for Lori. Especially at this time in your life. I can't imagine how hard it has been for you, yet you've been such a friend to her." She stopped again for a moment and took both my hands into hers. "Lori means so much to us, to me. Thank you."

She disappeared down the hall before I could respond. I sure didn't feel like much of a friend. I felt angry with myself for having done nothing to stop Gretchen, and at the same time I wondered what I really could have done.

I watched Megan fuss over Lori all evening, and it made me miss my own mother so badly my heart ached. I ended up leaving pretty soon after dinner. I wanted to be supportive, but there was only so much I could take. Driving home I thought about how everyone was so excited. Lori was literally glowing, and Megan was smiling and crying the whole time. I couldn't imagine what it would be like to lose my whole family and then, five years later, to be given a brand-new one.

God loved her an awful lot.

My throat got tight and my eyes stared to burn.

If God loved me, why would He take my mom away? How could He let that happen? I could feel the tears warm and wet on my face, the salty taste in my mouth. I pulled the car into a strip mall parking lot, and right there next to the Subway, I began sobbing.

I sobbed until there was nothing left inside of me except some tired hiccups. My face felt hot and swollen. I knew I needed to get home, but I couldn't move. I sat there forever. My mind was exhausted and blank.

At some point I turned the car back on and drove home on autopilot. I thought I was done, but when I walked into the kitchen and saw my dad working at the table, I started crying all over again. He jumped up from the table, his eyes wide and scared.

"Are you okay? What's wrong? What happened?" he asked, crossing the room in two steps.

I couldn't speak. I just collapsed into his arms and sobbed until my ribs ached. When it was all over and the hiccups had returned, I realized that we were both sitting on the kitchen floor, my dad leaning against the stove and me on his shoulder. His blue pin-stripe shirt was wet and wrinkled, but I felt so warm and safe that I didn't want to move.

"Are you okay?" he ventured after a while.

"Yeah. I guess so." My throat and mouth felt dry and raspy, but I didn't want to get up to get anything to drink.

"What happened, Butterfly?"

"I don't know. I was over at Lori's, and everybody was so happy and everything, and when I was driving home I started wondering why . . ."

"Why what?" he urged.

"Why God would take Mom away. Why would He do that if He really loved us? Didn't He know we needed her?"

I didn't have any more tears left in me. In their place was indignation. *How could He?*

My dad didn't answer for a while. And when he did, his voice sounded raspy too.

"Of two things I am very sure. I am very sure that God loves us, each of us, completely and fully. And I am very sure that I don't know why God allowed that accident to happen. We may never know why."

"How can you believe that? If He really loved us, He would have protected her. Right?" I asked.

"No. Not necessarily. We're not the first family to lose someone, and we won't be the last. It hasn't been easy. And I'm still sad. But I've made my peace with God about it."

"I've heard you say that before, but I don't know what you mean."

"It just means that I love God, even if I don't always understand Him." He took a deep breath and blew it out slowly.

"But how did you do it? I feel mad and sad all at the same time. I can't stop thinking that He shouldn't have let it happen. He should've made that guy be on some other road, some other night. Not on the road that would kill Mom."

He squeezed me tighter. "I know it's hard. And God understands that. It's just going to take time. You see, I had years to get to know God before the accident. I learned about who He was, and I learned that He loved me even though I didn't deserve it. But you, you're trying to get to know God knowing full well that horrible things still happen—even to good people. It'll just take time. But I'll help any way I can."

"I'm glad you're here. I guess it could have been worse. I could've lost you too."

He didn't say anything; we just sat there on the floor for a while longer.

"Why are you sitting on the floor?" Anna came around the counter and stood with her hands on her hips, looking at us as if we were crazy.

Dad smiled sadly. "We're just sitting here missing Mom."

She sat down on the floor in front of us, crossing her legs and smoothing her dress over her knees.

"But why are you sitting on the floor?" she persisted.

"This is just where we ended up, I guess," I told her.

"Oh." She stopped and thought for a moment. "I miss Mom too."

And there we sat. My sister, my dad, and I all sat on the kitchen floor, quietly missing Mom in our own private way. I mostly thought about the way she sounded, her voice, her laugh. I could still hear it inside. I had always felt that I missed out on knowing her because I pushed her away. But I did know her. Maybe not as well as I could have. But I knew that she loved to garden because it reminded her of her grandmother. I knew that she kept her hair long because it got all bushy and curly if she cut it too short. And I knew that she loved me. Even with all my mistakes and teenage attitudes.

I still craved her presence, though. Especially now that I didn't need to hide anything from her. Well, not anything really big. I might even have been able to talk to her about Gretchen . . . and Mark.

Mark. What was I going to do? I couldn't tell my dad about it. He'd overreact. And I'd have to admit that we had been seeing each other without seeing each other. Why did Mark have to make my life more complicated than it already was? And even the things that should be simple—like needing to boot Gretchen out of my life— weren't simple at all because of the consequences.

I looked at Anna and wished that I were eight again.

It was so much easier back then. It didn't seem that way then, of course, but I knew better now. Anna hadn't yet faced middle school, but with her outspokenness—and her disregard for what other kids thought—I didn't think she'd have too many problems.

That's when it hit me. Maybe that's all that made Gretchen different. She had confidence when the rest of us were feeling insecure—about our bodies, our selves, and our place in the social sphere. And so we followed her. Anna had the same "go my own way" attitude that Gretchen did. I could only hope that Anna would wield her power more gently than Gretchen did.

* * *

When I crawled into bed that night, I knew in my head that my crying jag hadn't solved anything, and it certainly didn't change the fact that my mother was gone, but somehow I felt just a little bit different. Like a room in my heart had been opened up and cleaned out of its cobwebs and debris. I felt better, but later I wondered how many rooms were still locked up.

 into the water below and watch it disappear into the pool of water. My legs dangle over the edge, moist from the waterfall mist. I close my eyes, lie back onto the warm rock, and let the sun paint me with light.

"So, Beka. What do you think you should do?" Her voice is soft and warm. I squint open my eyes to look at her, her long auburn hair glinting red in the sun.

"I don't know. That's why I want to know what you think."

She laughs softly. "Oh, I see. Don't want to have to work for the answer?" She reaches over and pokes my ribs gently, making me laugh.

"Well," she says, leaning back on her elbows and letting her hair sweep the rock underneath. "Maybe you should think about . . ."

*   *   *

"Beka? Beka!" Dad's voice finally broke through.

"What? What?" I sat up in bed, panicked and then immediately mad. "Mom was just about to tell me what to do," I moaned. "Whatd'ja have to wake me up for?" I flopped back on the bed. Now how could I get back into that dream?

"Sorry, Beka, but I think you overslept. Don't you have a rehearsal today?"

Now that woke me up. I looked at the clock and groaned.

"Oh no. Oh no. I've only got twenty minutes to get there. I have to be on time. Thompson's going to kill me."

"I'm sure he'll understand," Dad said.

I shot him a look. He obviously did not know Mr. Thompson.

He lifted his arms in surrender. "Okay, I'll leave you to get ready. Let me know if I can do anything to help you."

"You wanna be Annie's understudy?" I yelled after him.

"Very funny," he answered from the stairway.

I flew toward the bathroom. I wasn't even going to have time to wash my hair.

*   *   *

I ran onto the stage seven minutes late. I had made record time and was completely out of breath, but it didn't spare me any embarrassment.

"You're late," Thompson snapped when I sat down on the stage.

"Sorry." It came out like a croak.

I caught my breath and tried to relax as he gave his rehearsal notes to everybody. It was his chance to tell everybody what they were doing wrong. We only had two weeks left before the performance, and his notes were getting pickier. He wanted everything to be perfect.

We ran through some of the more difficult scenes and rehearsed all of the dances. Thompson had me doing double duty since I worked on some scenes as Molly and some as Annie, plus I had to make sure I knew the dances as both characters. It was still hard for me to remember who I was supposed to be when. By the end of the morning I felt like I had been turned inside out.

*   *   *

While I was walking to my car, I heard Mark's voice calling, "Wait up!" I couldn't help but get a thrill. The attention was very satisfying. So I turned around and smiled.

"Hey!" he said when he caught up with me. "I wanted to tell you that you looked great up there today. Actually, you'd make a better Annie than Gretchen."

"Don't say that. I'm not going to be Annie. Gretchen would never allow it."

"Still. For someone who has never done this before, I'm impressed. And you're a better singer than anyone up there."

I could feel my cheeks growing hot. The more I tried not to blush, the more I blushed.

He grinned but was kind enough not to comment on my red cheeks. "By the way, what are you doing tonight?"

"I don't know yet. Why?"

"We're having a concert at our church tonight."

"Oh, I heard about that. My friend Nancy mentioned it at church."

"Do you want to come?"

What did that mean? I didn't know how to answer, because I didn't know if he was just inviting me to his church or if he was inviting me to come *with him.* Why did everything have to be so confusing?

"Who else is going?" It was the only question I could think to ask to get a better feel for what he was really asking. I wanted it to be a date. Even after the waterfall incident I still liked him. My brain definitely felt mushier when he was around.

"Well, it's open to anybody, so it won't just be kids from my church."

That's not what I mean! I frantically tried to think of an intelligent thing to ask so that I wouldn't embarrass myself.

He reached down and took my hand in his.

"C'mon. I'd really like you to come."

"But I thought you said . . ." I was really getting confused.

He pulled me close enough to him that I could smell just a hint of cologne.

"I know. I said we couldn't date. And it won't be a date. Not technically. Just come and be with me."

"Isn't that kind of what a date is?"

"Yeah, but if we don't call it a date, then we don't have to jump through all the hoops that go with it."

Now I knew what he was saying, but I wasn't sure I liked it. He was standing close enough that I felt really good and really uncomfortable all at the same time. I wondered what my breath smelled like.

"It sounds pretty dishonest to me."

"We don't have to lie about it. We're just spending time together as friends, right?"

His hand in mine and his other one around my back didn't exactly feel like friendship. But it felt good too. I should have argued with him. But I wanted to be near him. To have his attention. And if that's the way he wanted it, I could live with it.

"Well, then maybe I should bring Lori with me tonight. If I come."

"Bring whoever you want. As long as you come." He leaned down and kissed me on my cheek. "It starts at seven."

And then he was gone. He walked away toward the other end of the parking lot. When I reached my car, I just leaned against it, trying to get hold of my whirling emotions. I closed my eyes and turned my face toward the noon sun. It stunk that I was getting what I wanted in a way that seemed wrong. It spoiled it somehow.

"Oh—my—goodness!" A voice broke me out of my thoughts.

Gretchen had pulled her car up next to me. She climbed out of it and stood in front of me. "Why didn't you tell me! I can't believe you'd keep this from me!"

"What?" I knew exactly what she was talking about.

"You and Mark! You looked awfully cozy over here. So, details. What's going on?"

"Nothing's going on." *At least technically.*

"Oh, please. That did not look like nothing to me."

"Were you watching?" I asked.

"Yeah, I was parked over there. I just waited until you were done with your moment before I came over."

"We're friends. That's all. And please don't tell anyone else." I didn't want the whole school whispering about us when the "us" was still so questionable.

"Well, you should have told me you two were secretly seeing each other. Especially since you have me to thank."

"You?" My heart tightened. Did she set this up? Was Mark only doing it because Gretchen told him to? The questions tumbled around inside of me.

"The spell. Remember?" Gretchen whispered.

"You put a spell on him?"

"Hello? We don't need the whole school knowing about our sisterhood."

I looked around the empty parking lot. "There's no one here, Gretchen. Why would you do that?"

"That's what friends are for, Beka. I knew you were a little nervous about it, so I went ahead and did it for you. And it worked! I'm so psyched. Hey, come with me. Let's go down to the bookstore and find some other spell books. There's this great little New Age shop downtown."

I hesitated. "I should get home."

"C'mon. It won't take long. And I'll buy you lunch. Pleeeeeease?"

Gretchen was fun to be around when she was being

friendly like this. I didn't want to put her in a bad mood by refusing to go. So I climbed into the car with her, and fifteen minutes of comparing Jason and Jeremy later, we pulled up in front of a store downtown.

*   *   *

"Can I help you ladies with anything?" A woman wearing a short printed skirt and oversized sweater came out from behind the counter. Her dark hair was cropped short, and she wore some simple jewelry around her wrists and neck. She seemed pretty normal looking, except for maybe the bare feet. I had expected some hippie with long flowing robes and a headdress.

"We're just looking around right now," Gretchen said, pulling me toward some bookshelves at the back of the store.

"Let me know if I can help," she said as she returned to her stool.

Gretchen dropped to her knees in front of the shelf and began pulling down books and flipping through them.

I looked around. We were in a little alcove, with three bookshelves lining the walls, at the rear of the store. In the main part of the store there were all sorts of other stands and racks. I walked back up, flipping through the greeting cards and looking through the jewelry cases. There were lots of crystals, but also lots of dragons and other medieval-type figures made in silver. I stopped when I got to the next case. It had several crystal balls in it. I never realized that people actually used those things.

"Would you like to see one?" The lady went behind the case and began to unlock it.

"No." I shuddered. The whole store gave me the creeps.

"They work, you know. When you know how to use them," she said.

"Yeah, sure."

"A skeptic, huh? Well, we all learn in our own time. It looks like your friend is embracing the truth." She looked back at Gretchen for a moment and then fixed her eyes on me.

"The truth? This is all just for fun. Isn't it?"

"No, this is all very real. I wouldn't even be here if it weren't for my spirit guide. She saved my life."

"Well, Jesus saved mine," I blurted out. I wished I had more practice talking about God. I thought again about how I needed to read the Bible more so I wouldn't sound like an idiot when I tried to say something about Him.

"Oh, is Jesus your spirit guide?"

"No. I mean . . . what?"

"Your spirit guide," she repeated. "The one who walks with you to help you and guide you."

"Well . . . He's not a spirit guide. He's Jesus. I mean, He does help me and . . ." I looked at Gretchen's back, hoping she'd rescue me from the conversation, but she was still absorbed with the books.

"Oh, you're one of those." She moved away from the cabinet. "One of those people who think that their truth is all there is. You're young, though, and naive. Maybe you can still learn to be open-minded."

"But . . ." I began to protest, but she was walking

away, and I didn't know what to say anyway. I felt all mixed up.

"Look what I found." Gretchen came up and shoved a book in my hand.

"You're too late."

"Huh?" she said. "Look at these. This one is all about harnessing your divine power. Isn't that cool?"

"Not really. Can I have the keys? I'm going to wait in the car."

"Fine. Be a killjoy. I'm going to go buy these."

I left the store, the wind chimes on the door tinkling as I did. I climbed into her Jeep and leaned back on the seat. I had no real idea what the lady had been talking about, but I was disturbed that I couldn't articulate what I believed. I did believe in Jesus. Believed that He had died for my sins. I even believed that He was alive and with me. How that was different from a spirit guide I didn't know. I just knew that it was different.

"Check these out." Gretchen tossed a plain paper bag onto my lap as she backed out of her parking space. I didn't open it. I just sat there as she drove back onto the street.

"What were you talking to that lady about?" she asked.

"I have no idea. Something about spirit guides. She was bizarre."

"Spirit guides? I read about those somewhere. I'm going to name mine Diana, after the goddess of love."

"You make it sound like a pet."

"It's not a pet. It's more like an invisible force that helps you in life."

"Okay, so it's an imaginary friend."

"Spirits are very real, Beka. You should know that. The Bible talks about all kinds of spirits."

"I don't think you and the Bible are talking about the same thing." Actually, I was sure of it. I just couldn't prove it.

"Hey!" Gretchen shouted as she slapped her hand on the horn for a second time. "That guy just cut me off. What a . . ."

"Look out!" I could barely get the words out of my mouth as I saw the white van pull out in front of us. Gretchen was going too fast to stop. She swerved to her right. Hard. I grabbed on to the dashboard to keep my balance.

"Oh no!" Gretchen yelled.

I could feel the right tires lifting off the pavement. We seemed to teeter that way for a long time. Then gravity won and the Jeep rolled onto its side and then seemed to keep rolling. When it stopped, all I could see was grass.

I looked over at Gretchen. Her eyes were open and she was staring at the ceiling of the Jeep. We both were dangling upside down by our seat belts. I could feel the strap digging into my abdomen. I felt nauseous all of a sudden.

"I think I'm going to throw up," I said to her.

"Don't you throw up in my car."

"Gretchen, take a look. I don't think you'd even notice." The windshield was smashed, with nothing but grass and mud where it once was. I looked out the passenger side windows, but there was also grass and mud.

"Where are we?"

"I think we're in a ditch," she said.

It felt like we had stopped in the middle of a roller-coaster loop. My muscles were beginning to tremble from keeping them in place. The seat belt was really hurting.

"Should we unbuckle ourselves?" I asked.

"We'll land on our heads in all that." She pointed at the grass, mud, and safety glass strewn all over the ceiling. Her curly red hair looked twice as big as usual. Normally, it would have struck me as funny. But it didn't seem funny just then.

"It's better than hanging here. This is really hurting my stomach."

"Are you okay?" she asked. "My stomach feels okay."

"I don't know. I guess so. It just hurts. I'll probably be fine after I get this belt off. I'm going to unbuckle it." I didn't care if I landed on my head. I had to get that belt off. Now.

*   *   *

"You okay in there?" A gruff voice yelled into the Jeep after someone thumped on the metal.

"Get us out of here. I think my friend's hurt," Gretchen yelled. I was touched. She actually cared.

"We'll get you out. Hang tight."

"Ha-ha. Not funny," I muttered.

*   *   *

I wasn't sure how long it took them to get us out. It felt like forever. When they did, the fireman helped me up out of the ditch and walked me over and sat me on the back of the ambulance so the paramedics could look me over. They poked and prodded, but I didn't even think I had hit my head. I kept saying I was okay to everyone who asked, but I still felt very trembly and nauseous. Gretchen was being looked at in the other ambulance. I looked around at all the rescue vehicles, police cars, and fire trucks. All this fuss.

"Miss? Are you feeling okay?" A police officer came over to me.

"I think so." I rubbed my stomach.

"I'm Detective Jarrell. Can you tell me what happened?"

I stood up to show him where the accident happened, and the whole world, all the lights and people and cars, all started spinning. I couldn't feel my knees underneath me, and then suddenly I threw up. All over Detective Jarrell's left shoe.

I felt better after that.

I told him what had happened, how a car had cut us off and that a van had pulled in front of us. I didn't tell him that Gretchen was going too fast, and I certainly didn't tell him that she didn't see the van because she was yelling at the car that had cut us off. I tried hard to make it sound like it wasn't Gretchen's fault.

I borrowed a phone from one of the paramedics, who were now insisting that I go to the hospital. I didn't want to scare my dad by letting someone else phone him. If I called, he'd know that I was okay.

*   *   *

By six, Dad and I were driving home from the hospital. They couldn't find anything to worry about; they just told me to take Motrin for any achiness. Dad had been great at the hospital. Paul, Lucy, and Anna had come too, but what really freaked me out was that Dad's friend Gabby had showed up. She didn't stay very long, but it bothered me to no end that my dad had called her and told her about the accident. He had promised that they were just friends and that he hoped she might be able to help us with "girl things," but if that was true, why would he call her at a time like that? She even brought flowers, which felt like bribery to make me like her or something. I took them, but I still felt angry with Dad about it. By the time they released me, only Dad was left. I was still mad, so as we drove home I was trying to find a way to ask him what he was thinking when he called Gabby. But I just couldn't bring myself to do it. I think part of me just didn't want to know.

"Dad? Can I ask you something?"

"Sure, sweets. What's on your mind?"

"I was going to ask you earlier, and then all this . . . Well, I was wondering if I could go to a concert at one of the other churches tonight. It's that brick one out on Marlin Road."

"Tonight? I don't think so. You were just in a car accident, Beka."

"I'm fine."

"But you should rest, stay off your feet."

I resisted the urge to whine. I knew whining wouldn't go over very well anyway, so I chewed on the insides of my mouth to resist the urge to complain. I was bummed. I felt fine and didn't want to waste the whole evening lying on the couch.

Dad glanced over at me several times before he spoke. "Is it that important to you?"

"Yeah."

"I hate for you to miss it, but I'm worried about you."

"I'll take it easy. I'll even stay in my seat. And if anything starts hurting, I'll come home. Please?"

"All right. If you promise to stay off your feet. But you're not driving. Paul or I will drive you over."

"Fine. That's fine. And I can probably get a ride home afterward."

"Well, if you can't, you can call us."

My anger had given way to pure joy. Mark Floyd, here I come.

*   *   *

Since it had gotten so late, I rushed, ever so gently, to get ready in time. I had called Lori with a last-minute invitation to come with me, which her parents had agreed to. I wanted to be with Mark, but it would feel weird if I just showed up all by myself.

I decided casual was the way to go, choosing dark jeans and a green short-sleeved sweater. People were always telling me that I looked good in green, and that it brought out my eyes. I hoped they were right. I put a little bit makeup on, which did nothing to cover my freckles but did make my face look better.

While I was tying my hair up, I began to notice how sore my shoulders and back were feeling. But it didn't even cross my mind to stay home. I was downstairs and ready to go in plenty of time.

Paul was standing in the kitchen.

"Wow, you look nice," he said. *Yes! Now if I can just get that reaction from Mark . . .*

"Thanks. You driving me? We have to pick up Lori, you know."

"I know. We better get going."

We walked to the car, and Paul drove toward Lori's house with my directions.

"I'm going to stay for the concert too."

"You are?" I instantly felt ill again. I had thought he would just drop me off, but if he was going to be there, then he was going to see Mark, and that would probably not go over very well. Paul was a good brother, and he took protecting his sisters seriously. Since I had never had boyfriends or anything, I had never gotten to see him in action. But I could imagine. Paul would stand between Mark and me like a pit bull. My only hope was that maybe there would be so many people there, he wouldn't watch me too closely. He was really going to put a crimp in things tonight.

"Why? That's not a problem, is it? I heard one of the band's CDs, and they sounded great. Besides, I could use a night off."

Besides his regular senior year schoolwork, Paul was taking a college class at the community college to get a jump on his general education requirements. I felt that heavy feeling inside as I thought about him going away in the fall. Even though he acted like a second father sometimes, I knew I was going to miss him. I pushed the thought away. I didn't want to be dwelling on depressing things when I was going to see Mark.

Lori came running out of the house when we pulled in her driveway. She looked stunning as usual, in a bright purple sweater and black skirt, her dark hair pulled back from her face and wrapped with a purple scrunchie.

"Ohh, this is going to be fun. Thanks for calling me!" she said as she climbed into the backseat. "And thanks for picking me up, Paul."

"No problem," Paul said.

Lori and Paul made small talk on the drive over, leaving me to imagine what the evening would be like. The revelation that Mark had actually slept with that girl still bothered me. But it didn't bother me enough to not want to be near him. His smile, his attention, everything else about him drew me and made me want to be close. I had never felt this way before, so the excitement of it all was so tied up with my emotions that I couldn't sort out one from the other.

I didn't want to sneak around about it, though. I knew I could get rid of that guilty feeling if I just told my dad about it and did the whole thing right. But if Mark wasn't willing to do that, what choice did I have? It wasn't hurting anybody, and maybe I could convince Mark to talk to his parents so we wouldn't have to be secretive.

When we pulled into the packed parking lot, a thrill surged through me. With so many people, Paul would be occupied. Maybe he wouldn't even notice that I was hanging around with Mark.

We parked and went inside. The foyer was full of

teenagers and several adults, and there were tables set up along the wall with T-shirts, CDs, and all sorts of other things to look at. Paul told us he'd see us later, and he disappeared into the darkened sanctuary, which already had music pumping from inside of it. Lori and I looked at the tables for a few minutes. I kept looking around for Mark, but I didn't see any sign of him. I was glad Lori was there, because I really didn't recognize anybody. If I had come by myself, I doubt I would have stayed.

"Are you going to buy a CD?" Lori asked.

"Maybe afterward, if I like the music." I flipped the CD over to look at the song titles. There was one named "Secrets." How apropos.

"Let's go and check it out then. It sounds pretty cool."

"Let's wait a few minutes," I said, hoping to give Mark just a little longer to appear. Lori looked like she was going to ask why, but she turned back toward the CDs instead.

I was getting ready to give up when I thought I saw him down the hallway. I moved to the right a few feet to get a better look. People kept moving in front of me, but there was no doubt it was him. And he wasn't alone.

CHAPTER **18**

Becoming Beka   BECOMING BEKA

Lori came up beside me and followed
my gaze down the hallway.

"Who are you . . . oh. Who's that girl?" Lori asked.

"I don't know." I didn't know whether to cry or yell.
A girl with long blonde hair was leaning on the wall, her
hands behind her, and she was talking to and smiling at
Mark. For his part he was leaning with one hand on the
wall just above her shoulder, looking down at her, smiling right back. Everything about their posture screamed
couple. I was frozen. I didn't know what to do or think. It
couldn't be what it looked like. He had wanted me to
come.

"Did you know he was going to be here?"

"Yeah, it's his church. He invited me."

"So why did you bring me?"

I broke my stare down the hallway and turned to Lori. She looked hurt.

"Mark said it was a concert, open to the public, and it's not a date or anything. I thought you'd like it. I'm sorry. I didn't mean to . . . I should have told you what was going on. Not that it matters at this point." I looked back down the hallway at Mark, who was still thoroughly absorbed in his pretty blonde.

"Let's just go in and see the concert," she said.

"I can't."

"Yes you can. He's obviously busy right now."

"But you don't understand. When we talked this morning, he . . ." Tears sprang into my eyes. I didn't really want to try to explain myself. Lori looked at me, waiting for me to finish, but I honestly didn't know how to explain it.

Then Mark looked toward me and our eyes locked. He seemed surprised for a minute and then smiled widely.

"He just saw me," I told Lori through my teeth.

"Beka, I'd just forget about him. Haven't you seen enough?"

I didn't answer her, but I knew I couldn't just forget him. He had wrapped himself around my heart somehow. I couldn't just let go. But I was mad. He started walking toward me, leaving the blonde right there on the wall. Lori quietly moved away toward the tables. I was grateful for her sensitivity.

"Hey, Beka. You made it." He reached down for my hand, but I pulled it away. "What's wrong?" he asked.

"What's wrong? Who's the girl you were talking to? You seemed pretty cozy."

"What? Oh, her." He looked back down the hallway. "That's Stacy. She's just a friend from church." He reached down for my hand again, and this time I let him take it. I was still mad.

"A friend like we're friends? How many 'friends' do you have, Mark?"

"You're not jealous, are you?" He grinned, and I wanted to hit him. He looked around for a minute and then pulled me with him down the hallway opposite from the one he was just in. He tried two doors before one finally opened into a Sunday school room. We went inside.

"Look, Beka. I meant what I said to you. I want to be with you right now, but I'm not allowed to. If people see me with just you, they're going to assume we're together, and it's going to get back to my parents. I'm telling you, if I blow it again, they're going to ship me away from here. You don't want that, do you?"

"No. But it looked like . . ."

"It doesn't matter what it looked like. You're the one I want to be with. Stacy and I are just friends. Promise."

"But how do I know you're not telling her the same thing?" My anger had dissipated, leaving behind sadness and a bit of fear. He wrapped his arms around me and pulled me closer.

"Would I lie to you?"

I didn't know how to answer that.

He smiled again. "Can I kiss you?"

Most of me wanted to scream Yes! but something in

me said that it wouldn't be right. "No, you can't. When this stops being a big secret, I'll reconsider, but for now, if you can't commit anything to me, why should I commit anything to you?" I could hardly believe what I was saying. It was like someone else was saying the words.

He stepped back just slightly. "Okay, I understand. But can we still spend time together? I really do want to be with you."

"Let's just take it one step at a time. Maybe your parents will reconsider or something." I hoped they would anyway. I felt right about what I was saying, but it would be hard to stick to . . . especially when he smiled at me.

"Well, let's go watch the concert. We'll talk about this later, okay?"

I didn't answer, but I let him lead me out the door. We didn't even reach the sanctuary doors when he yelled, "Hey, Steven! You made it, man!" He turned toward me and said, "I'll be right back." He headed off toward the guy named Steven and some other guys. I felt like an idiot standing there. Then, a few minutes later, he disappeared into the sanctuary with Steven's group. I didn't even know what to think.

I looked around for Lori for several minutes before I spotted her. She was talking to a tall guy with dark hair, and she was smiling. I didn't want to interrupt. Besides, I got that pang of jealousy again; she just walked in and already had the attention of a cute guy. Lori had it easy.

I began to wander toward the bathroom when I heard Lori call my name. I turned around and tried to smile. I don't think it worked very well, but I walked toward her anyway.

"Beka, this is Brian. Brian, Beka," Lori said when I got there.

"Hi. I think we met at Mark's New Year's Eve party, didn't we?" I asked.

"Briefly, I think. It's great you guys came tonight. It's a bigger turnout than we expected," Brian said. Even though I knew he was a junior like us, he seemed older, with an olive complexion, short dark hair, and a chiseled jawline. "Do you all want to go in and listen?"

It was evident he wanted to stay with Lori, and I suddenly felt like a fifth wheel.

"Yes, let's," Lori said. She and Brian headed for the sanctuary and I tagged along behind. At least I wouldn't have to make conversation—the music would make it impossible. Lori and Brian kept moving into the darkness, but I hovered near the doorway. I had to think.

I couldn't see Mark, but I assumed he was mingling with his friends, having a good time, while I felt like a pigeon waiting for him to throw me a morsel. I thought about Gretchen, who had her guys move like puppets on a string. If they didn't please her, then they were history. I didn't want to be like that, but I felt like I was waiting for Mark to make a decision instead of deciding what was right for me.

Was Mark right for me? I wasn't sure I really wanted to ask the question, much less answer it.

"All alone?"

I turned, expecting Mark to be standing there, and instead found Josh, dressed in a blue polo shirt and slacks. The blue made his eyes sparkle even in the dim light.

"I guess." It was hard to concentrate on what to say with him smiling at me.

We stood there for a few minutes, and I pretended to listen to the music since that's what it looked like he was doing.

Josh said something that I couldn't quite make out, and when I asked what he had said, he instead gestured out toward the foyer.

"It's quieter out here, if that's okay," he said when we had moved away from the open doors and the music.

"No, that's fine." I followed him over to a cushioned bench seat where we both sat down. He turned toward me and put his arm along the back of the seat, so I turned slightly toward him as well. I felt awkward. I had only met him that one time at his house. I couldn't imagine why he wanted to sit and talk with me.

"Is Nancy here?" I asked.

"No. She was going to come, but she's not feeling well."

"Oh, I'm sorry."

"Oh, she'll be fine. She hardly ever gets sick, but when she does, she's down for days. Must be in her genes."

"Yours too, I suppose."

"Well, she's my sister, but not genetically."

"Huh?"

"We're both adopted. Didn't you know that?" he asked.

"No. I've only known Nancy for a few weeks. It never came up. But it does explain why you look so different from each other."

"Yeah." He laughed. "People don't say anything, but I know they wonder about it."

The conversation stopped for a moment. I tried to think of something to say. Nancy was a safe topic, but I couldn't come up with another question.

"So tell me your story," he said.

"My story?" I had lots of stories, but none I wanted to tell at that moment.

"Yeah, how did you get to know Jesus?"

I had never really been asked that question, and I certainly had never been asked a question like that by an adorable-looking guy in a rather public place.

"Don't you know? I mean, hasn't Paul . . ." I felt all flustered. I knew he was friends with Paul, and I had just assumed he probably knew my sordid history.

"Paul shares stuff about himself, but he's quiet about his family, except to ask for prayer maybe. He did tell me about you getting things worked out with God, but no details—I think he was so excited that it just slipped out. He really is very protective of you. In fact—" he looked around—"if he catches me with you, I'll have to answer to him." Josh grinned.

My heart fluttered when he said that, partially because of Paul and partially because of Josh. I thought about Mark and wondered what he would say if he saw me sitting there with Josh. I even began hoping he'd come out—it would serve him right. What a bad attitude! But I couldn't help it.

A lot of kids and adults were milling around, but I doubted that anyone would hear me. Even so, I had no practice at telling what had happened to me. Josh sat patiently while I tried to make myself start speaking.

"Well, my family thought I had accepted Christ when I was thirteen, but I didn't really until just this past December."

"Sounds like there's an interesting story in between. Do you want to share it?"

I shrugged.

"You don't have to. I'm just curious about you."

I wanted to ask why, but I wasn't sure I wanted to hear the answer. I wondered if maybe Josh was just being friendly, or if there was more going on.

"You can trust me," he added. "I know you don't know me, but I'm not the type of guy to repeat what I hear. Though I might encourage *you* to share it with other people."

Lori was the only one who knew the whole story, and telling some guy I hardly knew, even if he was cute, felt weird. I wasn't ashamed of God being in my life, but I was ashamed of my choices, especially of feeling suicidal. And unfortunately, that was part of the story.

"How 'bout an easier question? You know Nancy and I are home-schooled, right? Well, the association we belong to is putting on a formal dance for all the home-schooled kids in our area. I wanted to know if you might be interested in coming with me."

I swallowed hard. I was sure he was talking about the dance that Lori was going to with Brian. I just got asked out. I could hardly believe it. I instantly wondered about Mark. We weren't dating, so it wouldn't be like cheating or anything, but would he see it that way? I thought about him smiling at that pretty blonde earlier, then abandoning me and not even noticing. It would serve him right. I blurted out, "I'd love to go. When is it?"

"Really?" He seemed genuinely happy that I had said yes, which seemed odd only because I was sure that just about anybody would have said yes to him. "It's at the end of April."

"Well, I'll have to ask my dad and see if it's okay, but I think it'll be fine."

"If your dad wants to meet me first, that's fine. I'll understand."

I had a feeling my dad would want to meet him, but I thought I'd save the worry over that for another time. Especially since Mark had just come out of the sanctuary and was headed right for us.

*　　　*　　　*

"There you are, Beka—I was wondering where you slipped off to." It ticked me off, because he was the one that had ditched me.

Mark turned his attention over to Josh and nodded at him. "Josh." Mark didn't say anything else, but his eyes were full of questions.

"Can I talk to you a minute, Beka?" Mark asked. Josh politely excused himself, and Mark immediately took his seat beside me. I felt like I was in an alternate reality. It couldn't be me that had two interested guys, could it?

"So, what's going on?" Mark wasn't smiling anymore.

"Nothing. Josh is sort of a friend."

"Sort of?"

"Yes. We just met. Why am I getting the third degree, Mark? We're just friends, remember?"

"That's the way it has to be, not the way I want it to be. What do you want?"

"Look, I just want something that I know what to call it. If we're friends, fine; if we're dating, fine. But I don't know what it is because you're saying we're friends while acting like it's more than that. It's too confusing." I tried to stand up, but Mark stopped me.

"What if I talk to my parents? What if they change their mind? Then what would you want?"

"I don't know. I really don't know."

*　　*　　*

Driving home, Paul was surprised and Lori was thrilled to hear about Josh asking me to the dance. I was quick to let Paul know that I knew I still had to ask Dad, but Lori was already planning a double date. I was pretty sure that Dad would be fine with it, but Paul's jaw was set, and I couldn't figure out what he was thinking.

"You're okay with that, aren't you, Paul?"

"Yeah," he said.

I didn't believe him. "You don't seem fine with it."

He glanced over at me and smiled sadly. "I guess it had to happen sooner or later. I just wasn't prepared for it."

I didn't say anything else about it, assuming that it was just a big brother thing. And even though Mark was still on my mind, I was looking forward to seeing Josh in the morning. It was exciting and confusing all at the same time. And I knew that eventually I would have to start making some decisions of my own.

I was still glowing from church when I got up on Monday morning. Not only did I leave there feeling closer to God than I had in a while; I had also seen Josh. He had made a point to talk to me after our Sunday school class was over. We talked about the class, and I told him about how during worship I felt this extraordinary sense of peace come over me. I hadn't intended to share that with him, but it came tumbling out of my mouth. He seemed happy for me.

One thing had struck me as I pondered church, and Josh and Mark. Even though I had only had a couple of conversations with Josh, he managed to bring up Jesus in every one of them. But Mark—Mark hadn't talked about

God since that New Year's Eve night, not even when he admitted that he had slept with that girl. It was easy to see that Josh loved the Lord, but I wasn't so sure about Mark.

Either way, I had felt so sure of God's love for me that I woke up Monday still feeling that peace. One of the things the special speaker in Sunday school had mentioned was how important it was to read the Word of God. I had not really been doing that, depending instead on church and class to carry me. The lady had said, "How can you expect to know God and follow Him if you don't know what He's saying to you?" I did want to follow God, but I could say that forever and never mean it unless I did something about it. Until yesterday I wasn't sure what to do about it. But reading the Bible every day was something I felt I could do. It would at least get me going in the right direction. And then maybe after the play was over I could join Lori's Bible study as well. I was excited about the prospects.

And then I got to school.

*   *   *

Gretchen was standing at my locker, looking annoyed. I took a deep breath and walked over to her.

"There you are! Cutting it a little close, aren't you?"

"I have time," I said. "Are you feeling okay? I mean, after the accident?"

"I'm fine. A little sore I guess. You?"

"Same thing. What about your Jeep?" I wanted to be polite, but I didn't really want to talk to Gretchen. She was spoiling my good mood.

"Oh, that. Dad got me a new one." I rolled my eyes. Only Gretchen. "By the way," she added, "you might want to check the bulletin board today." She sauntered off before I could say anything. After last week I was hoping Gretchen would just forget about that horrible story and move on. Apparently, I was wrong. And my good mood was gone.

*   *   *

I didn't bother pulling up the bulletin board since I knew what it would say, but I did ask Lori about it at lunch.

"It's just frustrating. Who would do this? I mean, it's ridiculous. Isn't it ridiculous?"

"Yes, completely." I wanted to tell her it was Gretchen. But admitting I knew who it was would also mean admitting that I knew about it—and failed to stop it in the first place. I felt bad, but Lori seemed to be doing okay.

"The worst part about it is that I have to pray for this person. Up until this morning I was doing okay with it, and now I'm upset all over again." She let out a big sigh.

"You mean the 'praying for your enemies' thing?"

"Yeah, Megan, uh . . . Mom was talking with me about it last week when all this started. She said the best thing I could do would be to pray for this person, and it really has been helping me. Obviously it's not doing much for them."

I thought about Lori praying for Gretchen. It was an odd thought.

"I thought I had really forgiven them," she continued. "But I guess I still have more forgiving to do, since this bothers me so much."

"Well, I don't blame you. It's pretty rotten."

"You know, I've heard people say that believing in God was like using a crutch in life—just something to believe in to make life easier. But the more I read the Bible, the more I realize just how crazy that is. I mean, the stuff God asks you to do is hard, so hard that He has to help us do it. Like my real mom. I always thought that I just felt sorry for her, but lately I'm starting to realize that I'm pretty angry with her. She blew it big time with me right when I needed her the most. Walking with God is wonderful, but it's not easy."

*   *   *

By seventh period, I had overheard several conversations about Gretchen's latest installment. It had been stripped off the board, of course, but plenty of kids had seen it and printed it off. I had even found one stuffed into my locker. I thought maybe Olive was still being framed, but she was sitting in journalism along with everybody else, looking more nervous than usual.

While I was typing on the computers, the loudspeaker in our room buzzed and a voice said, "Ms. Adams?"

"Yes," she answered.

"Could you please send Rebekah Madison to the principal's office?"

Ms. Adams said she would, then turned and looked

at me. Since it was almost time for dismissal, I slowly gathered up my books and backpack before leaving. Even though I knew I hadn't done anything, my stomach was churning violently. I had never been called down to the office without knowing what it was about. I was the good girl. I couldn't imagine why she needed to see me.

I told the secretary that I was there, and she told me to have a seat. I waited, opening and closing the zipper on my backpack until the secretary gave me a dirty look. I folded my leg up on the chair so that I could pick at my shoelaces instead. Anything to keep my mind off what might happen. The final bell rang, and the hall behind me filled with kids and then emptied within minutes. I was late for rehearsal. I briefly wondered if I should try to get a message to Thompson, and then decided I'd just have to explain later.

Eventually the secretary led me back to Mrs. Brynwit's office, and I sat down in one of the leather chairs. Mr. Irney, the vice principal, was also there. I felt like throwing up.

"Rebekah, do you know why you're here?" Mrs. Brynwit asked.

"No." It came out sort of like a croak. I cleared my throat so that I could answer better.

She handed me a piece of paper with Gretchen's third installment of the story printed out on it.

"You've seen this?" she asked.

"Yes." I wasn't about to add that practically everyone had seen it.

"Well, Rebekah. We have a serious problem. Why did you post such a thing?"

"What? Me? I didn't post that." It didn't take but a second to figure out why I was being accused.

"It originated from your log-in name and password. Why is that?" She was very calm, but I could tell she didn't believe me. "And Mrs. Palmer reported that you had been in to use the school computer lab earlier in the day. That's where this was uploaded from."

"I didn't post it," I repeated. "Someone else must have gotten my password and used it. Whoever did this used Olive's log-in too, right?" I was trying not to be rude, but I needed to convince them I wouldn't do something like that.

"You and Olive both work with *The Bragg About*, so you might have been able to discover her password during that time."

"If I did it and had someone else's password, why would I post it under my name so that I'd get caught?" I argued. I was pleased—it was a good point, though I wasn't sure how well I was able to articulate it.

"Because we changed Olive's information. So you didn't have another way to post it," she reasoned.

I groaned. How was I supposed to prove I didn't do it?

"I didn't do it. Lori's my friend. Ask her. She knows I would never do that to her. Or anybody else." It was a last-ditch effort.

"If you didn't do it, do you know who did?" she asked.

So far I didn't have to lie, but now, unless I gave up Gretchen, I was going to have to. Gretchen would know that it was me, and the consequences of that could be deadly.

"No." Even though I lied to protect her, I was mostly protecting myself.

"Well, for now, we will let you go until I talk to a few other people, including Miss Trent. But I'm afraid this isn't over until we get to the bottom of this."

*   *   *

I ran down the hallways to get to rehearsal and found them all onstage still warming up. I slipped into the back row and joined the voice exercises, still reeling.

Gretchen tried to talk to me a couple of times during rehearsal, but each time I managed to avoid her. I was ticked. It was terrible of her to do what she did to Olive, but me? I felt betrayed. I had trusted her, and she turned on me.

Mark was giving me looks all through rehearsal as if he wanted to talk to me too, but I wasn't ready to deal with him just yet. I did feel flattered, though, and my heart fluttered a bit more than I expected. I took off as soon as rehearsal was over and tried to get out of there before anyone caught up. But I wasn't quick enough for Gretchen.

"Hey!" She came running up to me, then stopped and smoothed her skirt and flipped her hair. "Really, Beka, you shouldn't make me run. It's so juvenile."

I didn't respond.

"So, what happened? Fill me in."

"As if you didn't know. How could you?"

"What? All you had to do was tell them it wasn't you, for goodness' sake. It was the best way to do it, because no one would believe that you would do it. Especially since you insist on being friends with that thing."

"Well, I don't think they believed me."

"You covered for me, didn't you?" Her eyes narrowed.

"Yes. But I shouldn't have."

"Oh, lighten up, Beka. It's all in good fun." She threw her arm around me and laughed. "And it is so fun!"

I moved away from her and went to unlock my car. She didn't seem to care that I wasn't laughing with her.

"Don't forget about Wednesday. We have an important meeting. Be at the meeting place right after rehearsal." She walked off toward her brand-new Jeep, and I started my little beat-up Corolla hatchback. That just about said it all.

By Wednesday nobody was even talking about the postings anymore, but I couldn't keep my mind off of them. I jumped out of my seat every time the room buzzer went off, thinking they were going to call me up again and kick me out of school.

"Don't worry about it. I'm sure they believe you," Lori said at lunch.

"I'm not sure. If I get suspended, then I'll miss the play. Not to mention spend the next six months locked in my room and walking everywhere."

"Let's not talk about it anymore. Oh, I got some good news at dance last night. Miss Haverty is putting me in two dances. The concert's coming up soon, though, so

I'm going to have to do some extra rehearsals to get ready in time."

"That's great." I tried to sound enthusiastic, but Lori wasn't buying it.

"The costumes are really beautiful too. The fabric for the scarves is this silky gold material, and then the body part runs across . . . well . . . It would be easier to draw it than describe it." She reached into her backpack. "I don't have my notebook with me. Do you have any paper?"

"Sure." I pulled out my journalism notebook and handed it to her.

She flipped it open, and some papers I had stuffed in there went sliding across the table. "What's this?" she asked, reading one of the papers. After just a moment she looked at me over the top of the paper. "Beka?"

"What?" I took the paper. It took me one second to realize it was the story Gretchen had made up about Lori, handwritten there on notebook paper.

"Did you . . . How could . . ." she couldn't finish her sentence, and her eyes had become glassy.

"Lori, it's not what it looks like. That's not my paper."

"Not yours? Then why do you have it? Even if this isn't yours . . . you knew about it; you knew it was going to happen." Her eyes darted around as she processed the discovery. I felt like disappearing into the floor. I tried to think of a way to explain myself. But either way, I looked rotten.

The bell rang, and we both just sat there, Lori looking stunned and me feeling guilty. Even though I hadn't done anything.

But I guess that was part of the problem. I hadn't done anything. I didn't stop it. And now not only had Gretchen hurt Lori, but I had too.

Lori slowly got out of her chair and took her backpack and tray. She left, her eyes wide and her lips silent. I wanted to call after her. To stop her and explain. But what was I supposed to say? I crumpled the paper in my hand, got my stuff, and left for class. On the way there I tossed the offending paper into the trash.

I was so preoccupied I walked straight into Mai, who was standing in the doorway.

"Oh, hi," I said.

"Beka." She said my name like it put a bad taste in her mouth. "Gretchen wanted me to remind you about tonight. She's not going to be here until rehearsal this afternoon."

"I know." I walked past her and wondered why she bothered to tell me. Gretchen would remind me at least twice more at rehearsal anyway. Besides, at that moment, I couldn't think about anything but Lori.

*　　　*　　　*

Thompson yelled at me twice during rehearsal, because I kept messing my lines up. I needed to get things straightened out with Lori quickly, or I was going to get kicked out of the play.

Gretchen reminded me three times over the course of the two-hour rehearsal, and by the third time I had almost told her I wasn't going to come. And I should have, but I was honestly afraid. It would be easier to go than to cause problems.

But while we were singing the last songs, which I knew cold at that point, I made a decision. Once the play was over with, and I didn't have to see Gretchen twelve hours a week, then I was going to have it out with her. I was going to put a stop to it before it went any further. I took a deep breath, feeling stronger just for thinking about standing up to her. I hoped the courage would last until I had to actually do it.

*   *   *

I was the first one at The Snack Shack, which figured. I didn't even want to be there, and I was standing around feeling stupid. But Liz showed up, followed by Mai and Gretchen soon after.

Gretchen opened the doors, and we all settled on the floor. She set up four candles around each of us before she said anything.

"Tonight we will make our vows to each other and to the gods that we will protect one another. We will call upon the forces of the earth to empower us and lead us toward spiritual enlightenment." She solemnly lit the four candles around her and passed the matches to Mai, indicating that she should do the same. Mai struck a match and lit her candles, then passed them to Liz. When Liz handed the matches to me, I held them for a moment.

"They're just candles, Beka. They don't bite," Gretchen said tolerantly.

I lit the candles, but I felt this gnawing deep inside of

me. I felt like running. I looked around at each of them as they waited for Gretchen to continue.

She took out a book and laid it open in front of her. "We'll do the vows at the end of the ceremony. You know, to seal everything, but we'll start with this spell. It will help us harness the divine power that is all around us. It won't just protect us, though; it will also give us power."

"What kind of power?" Liz asked.

"Any kind of power. But remember the threefold rule—anything you do will come back on you threefold," Gretchen explained.

"Well then, I guess you can expect some nasty rumors coming your way." The words bypassed my brain.

Gretchen ignored my comment. "Look, it's not wrong to take care of people who wrong us, as long as we don't do anything worse to them."

"And whose rule is this?" I asked.

"The universe's, Beka. Can we get on with this, please?"

I stopped talking.

Gretchen took a deep breath. "Okay, then. We need to purge this room of its negativity." She shot me a look and then turned and pulled a Ouija board out of her bag and unfolded it in the center of the circle. "Let's call upon the divine powers of the earth to . . ."

"Wait," I blurted out.

"What now?" Gretchen was mad now. But I didn't care. I didn't want to be a part of this whole sisterhood thing, and I knew that it was God who had power, not the earth. And I felt sick all of a sudden. Like if I stayed one moment longer, I would throw up or pass out or something. I thought about just leaving, walking out. I looked around the room at the candles and the board and suddenly remembered the verse I had read that morning, as clearly as if I had just read it. "'Therefore come out from them and be separate,' says the Lord. 'Touch no unclean thing, and I will receive you.'" I knew the passage was talking about believers and unbelievers. I knew what I had to do. *Lord, give me courage.*

"Gretchen, this isn't right. We can't be doing this. I won't do it."

"What is your problem, Madison?" Gretchen asked. Mai stared at me as if she was willing me to die right there. But I kept going.

"My problem is that all of this is crazy. There is a divine power, but it's not a goddess or a spirit guide. It's Jesus."

"You've got to be kidding. I thought you were over all that stuff. Grow up already."

"That's the thing, Gretchen, I finally figured it all out, and for the first time, I am growing up. Jesus really loves me, and I want to do what's right. Which this isn't. He loves you too. Come on. Let's just get rid of all of this stuff. God is what's real—not the earth or divine powers or any of that other mumbo jumbo."

Gretchen and Mai stared at me. Only Liz looked slightly relieved, but she didn't speak up to help out. I waited, wondering if I should say something else or just get up and leave.

"So, you're just too good for this. Is that it? You just

think you're so much better than everybody else." Gretchen spat the words out.

"No, not at all," I said. "I'm not good—that's the whole point. We all sin, so we all deserve to die. That's why Jesus came. He . . ."

"I'm not going to listen to this. You're either for us or against us, Madison. And I don't think I need to remind you what it's like having me for an enemy. You better choose wisely."

I didn't hesitate. I just stood up carefully and walked out of the little building and closed the door. I walked numbly across the soccer field and sat down on one of the team benches. I couldn't believe that I had walked out. God had answered my prayer—He had given me courage. I shivered. I looked across the field at The Snack Shack, thinking that I didn't want to be sitting here when they came out. But I couldn't move. My legs felt like lead, and my heart felt like it was trembling.

What had I done? I had chosen to make an enemy of Gretchen Stanley. On purpose. What was I thinking? I briefly thought about running back over and apologizing, but only for a split second. I knew I had done the right thing. There really wasn't another choice. Not if I really believed what I said I believed.

I wished I had a Bible with me so I could read that passage that had gotten stuck in my head. Did it really say that?

I closed my eyes and let the soft breeze blow across me, taking deep breaths. I didn't have anything to say to God, but I wanted to hear Him. I tried to clear my thoughts and just listen.

I don't know how long I sat there—I never could judge time very well, but when I opened my eyes, everything around me was still the same. But inside, I felt calm. I still dreaded the consequences, but I was sure that I had done what God wanted me to do. And I was sure that He was with me. It was enough for now.

I looked back over at The Snack Shack and wondered what they were doing inside. Just then I heard screaming. It was faint, and I thought maybe it was just some kids playing nearby. But as I listened more closely, it seemed to be coming from The Snack Shack.

I stood up and walked toward the building and then broke into a run. There was smoke pouring out of the cracks around the windows, and toward the right hand corner there were definitely flames.

I ran $around$ to the back of the building and turned the knob. It was locked. The screaming was loud and panicked now. I banged on the door.

"Unlock it. Quickly!" I shouted. The knob already felt warm, and smoke was pouring out from under the door.

All I heard was screaming, so I pushed at the door over and over, bumping it as hard as I could with my hip, but it wouldn't give way. *Lord, help me please. Help me open this door.* I ran away from the door and then ran back at it, throwing my left shoulder against it with all my might.

The door gave way, and I landed on the floor. All I

could see was smoke and the flames crawling up the front of the building. Gretchen, Mai, and Liz ran out the open door, coughing and sputtering. I crawled out after them, my shoulder throbbing.

"Are you okay? Are you guys okay?" I asked.

Liz nodded but kept coughing, sucking the air in hard.

Gretchen was the first to catch her breath. "Not a word about this to anybody. Understand? Make sure you shower and wash your clothes so no one smells the smoke. No one can know we were here." She had another coughing fit. When she stopped she said, "Let's get out of here." She ran off, still coughing, with Mai and Liz right behind her.

I stood there for only a moment and then ran toward the school, desperately trying to remember where the closest pay phone was. Did you have to pay to call 911? I couldn't remember.

I ran up to the one by the bus patio and quickly dialed 911. I didn't need to pay.

"Nine-one-one. What's your emergency?"

"Fire." I was out of breath. "There's a fire at the high school. At the athletic field."

"Okay, I'm dispatching the fire trucks. What's your name?"

I tried to think quickly. If I gave her my name, they would place me at the school. And I didn't have a good reason for being there. I hung up the phone and walked away from where I had just come. I figured if I went off the school property and then walked through the residential neighborhood to get my car, no one would think I had been anywhere near The Snack Shack.

I walked quickly, but not so fast as to draw attention. There were a few people in their yards, but I tried to seem occupied with my own thoughts. Just as I reached my car I heard the sirens. I climbed into my car and just sat there. My shoulder was still throbbing, and now my head was pounding.

*　　*　　*

It was bizarre that I got home to my normal house and family after what had just happened. They were just about to sit down to dinner. It was surreal.

"I'm glad you're home. Come and eat," Dad said after I had dropped my backpack in the hallway.

I slid into my seat and bowed my head for a moment since they had already prayed. I didn't have an appetite, so I pushed the food around my plate and listened to the conversation. After a while Dad asked me if I was all right.

"Yeah, just tired," I said. *And I just rescued three people from a burning building.*

"How's rehearsal going?" Paul asked.

"Fine. But I'll be glad when it's over. It's confusing having two parts."

"I imagine it is," Dad said.

After dinner I went upstairs to try to concentrate on my homework. I lay on my floor and stared at my chemistry book for about twenty minutes before there was a knock on my door.

"Can I come in?" Paul poked his head inside.

"Sure. I'm not getting anything done anyway." I closed my book and rested my chin in my hands. Paul sat down on the floor. "You look so serious. What's wrong?"

"Oh, nothing." He smiled. "Have you talked to Dad about Josh yet?"

I blushed. "No, not yet. The dance isn't until next month. I thought I'd wait until the play was over with."

"Oh." He got quiet.

"What is it?"

"Well, I don't have any problem with Josh. He's a great guy. And even though I'm not thrilled about you being with any guy, you couldn't do much better than Josh."

"I'm not with him or anything. It's just a dance."

"Oh, I know. But I'm worried about something else." He paused for a moment before continuing. "It's about Mark Floyd."

"Mark?" *Did he know about Mark?*

"Well, Josh mentioned that you two were talking, and he asked me if I knew anything about him. And I don't. I know he goes to our school, but beyond that, nothing. He only asked because he's concerned about you. That maybe you don't have all the information."

"What are you getting at, Paul? Spit it out." I was starting to get nervous. I didn't want Paul meddling before I had figured out what to do.

"Beka, I've just heard that Mark may not be on the up and up about some things."

"Like . . ."

"Like church. Josh knows Brian McKinley, the guy

who's taking Lori to that dance, from their home-school co-op."

"Yeah, so?"

"So, Brian and Mark go to church together. And he doesn't have the best reputation around there."

"Brian?"

"No, Mark."

"Tsk tsk. Should we be gossiping about other people? Really, Paul," I teased.

"I'm serious. I didn't even find out the details. I was just told that you should be careful."

"Oh." I thought for a moment. It could be the whole thing with that girl last summer that gave him a bad reputation, and he was honest enough with me to let me know about it. But I didn't want to tell Paul that little detail, because I doubted that would ease his mind.

"Well," I said, "I'll be careful. But we're just friends." Which was true and not true all at the same time.

"Okay. Fair enough. I just thought it was only right that I talk to you." Paul got up and left with a little wave of his hand.

Paul was always concerned with doing the right thing. If I could tell him how I did the right thing today without admitting that I did the wrong thing first, I would have. I wished I could tell today's story to someone.

Then I remembered how I left everything with Lori. With Gretchen and the fire I had completely put it out of my head, but now that sick feeling returned. I didn't really want to call her, since I wouldn't be able to see her facial expression. It was the kind of thing that I felt seeing her eyes would help me know what she was really feeling. But at the same time, I hated to wait until morning.

I had just started studying when suddenly there was pounding at my door. Lucy pushed open the door.

"Beka, come downstairs. You won't believe it." She disappeared, and I jumped up and ran down the stairs after her.

I found everyone in the family room watching the TV. I looked at the screen. A reporter was standing in front of what was left of The Snack Shack, a large pile of blackened wood, still smoldering.

"Nine-one-one dispatchers received a call at 5:45 P.M. alerting them to a fire at Bragg County High School. When fire crews arrived, there was little they could do to save the concession stand, which the booster club had named The Snack Shack. As you can see behind me, this is all that is left of the building. Early indications are leading investigators to believe that this fire was deliberately set. Police are looking for the 911 caller, who is described as a young female, and will be sorting through this rubble to find clues to the identity of the person or persons responsible for this. The Bragg County Boosters spent nearly twenty thousand dollars to build the concession stand two years ago. It will be a devastating loss to them. Back to you, Ray."

"Can you believe it? Who would burn down The Snack Shack?" Lucy asked.

"Somebody's going to get in big trouble, aren't they, Daddy?" Anna said.

"It looks that way. My goodness. They're going to

have to raise a lot of money to rebuild it." Dad shut off the TV, and I left to go back upstairs.

The police were looking for me? Would they be able to figure out that it was me who called? I shouldn't have been worried. After all, I had nothing to do with the fire, and I even rescued the three of them from it. They could have died in there. I should be a hero, and instead I was feeling sick and guilty.

I only had two choices—turn them in or pretend I didn't have anything to do with it. The problem was that I didn't know if the police would be able to track me down. And if they did, I couldn't lie to the police. I frantically thought about who had seen me. A few people had seen me in the area. Would they remember me? Would they be able to identify me?

I started to pray that they wouldn't figure out who I was, but I felt that probably wasn't a good prayer. So I just prayed for help—that God would get me through it. And that I wouldn't be so scared of what would happen. I reread the passage in 2 Corinthians about believers not being with unbelievers. I wasn't totally sure what "yoked" meant, but the gist of the passage was pretty clear. God had helped me do the right thing with Gretchen. I tried to keep that in mind, but the courage I needed now was so much bigger. And what I was facing was much scarier than just Gretchen.

I tossed and turned all night long, so I left for school feeling bleary and defeated. Pretty much every conversation I heard was about the fire. I didn't see Gretchen or Lori until second period, but when I did they both ignored me. I sat through the entire class feeling numb. When class was over Gretchen gave me a look that very clearly let me know that I was to keep my mouth shut.

The next couple of classes were a blur, and I was having lunch alone when Lori came and sat down across from me.

I looked up and tried to swallow the spaghetti in my mouth despite the lump in my throat.

"Hi," I said.

"Hi," she said flatly. "We need to talk."

I took a moment to wipe my mouth and my hands and then dropped my arms into my lap. I wasn't sure if she wanted to go first or if I should just jump in.

I decided to jump. "Lori, there isn't a good explanation for what happened, but there is an explanation." She sat silently but nodded. "Okay, I did not post that garbage on the bulletin board, but I did know about it. The person who did it showed me that paper you found a few days ago. I tried to talk them out of it, but I didn't get anywhere. I'm so sorry."

"It's Gretchen, isn't it?"

I nodded.

"Why?"

"She's mad because Jeremy asked you out."

"What? That wasn't my fault. And I said no anyway."

"I know. But trying to explain that to Gretchen is like trying to convince your English paper to type itself. Nothing worked. And she knew about the adoption too. She said she wouldn't tell anybody, but that I owed her. I thought if I pushed too hard she would do something even worse."

Lori sat quietly for a few minutes. I was getting nervous waiting until she gave me a small smile.

"I think I understand. And I forgive you."

I blew out the breath I had been holding. "Thank you. I know I don't deserve it."

"None of us do."

I felt so much relief that I almost laughed, but it came out more like a sob. The tears followed close behind.

"What's wrong? What happened?"

"I think I'm in trouble. You know that fire last night?"

Lori nodded, her eyes wide with worry and our problems apparently forgotten.

"I was there." I told her the whole story, whispering so that no one would overhear, starting with how Gretchen had gotten involved with the witchcraft right up to the fire. She nodded a lot and said "Oh my" several times.

"But, Beka, you didn't really do anything wrong. You're not responsible for the fire."

"I know, but I know who is. I'd have to turn her in."

"Yes. And?"

"And you know what Gretchen's like. I have a whole other year here. If I make it through this one. Gretchen will make my life miserable."

"Do you really think you can keep it a secret?"

"No." I knew I'd have to tell what I knew, but I didn't want to. If I had just gone home after I left, I wouldn't be in this mess.

But then Gretchen, Mai, and Liz might have died. As hard as this was, I wouldn't have wanted them to die. So I left the cafeteria, resigned to the idea that I would have to turn myself in.

*   *   *

At rehearsal, Gretchen was floating rumors about who started The Snack Shack fire. One thing I had to give her —she was a great actress. She was pretty convincing.

Other than our scenes together, Gretchen didn't speak

to me until the end of rehearsal, and when she did, she was mad as ever.

"You're welcome," I said with a smile on my face when she came up to me.

"For what?" she sneered.

"I think you know, Gretchen."

"Yeah, well, that's not the point of this conversation." She took out a folded piece of paper and handed it to me. "Just in case you're getting weak, I thought you should have all of the information." She turned and strode off. I watched as Mai came up to her, and they walked down the hallway laughing and talking. My stomach turned over. This event, no matter what I did at this point, was going to change the course of my life at high school. I didn't know if I was prepared for that.

I looked down at the note and slowly unfolded it. It had one sentence written on it: "Do you really want everyone to know where you were over winter break?"

I sucked in my breath as if I had been punched in the gut. How could she possibly know about the hospital? And if she did . . . I shook my head. *This can't be happening.* I didn't even know how to pray, what to say.

I walked slowly to my car, my mind spinning. The parking lot was almost empty. I saw Gretchen's Jeep toward the back of the lot. She was standing beside it with a guy. He was leaning on her as she leaned on the hood of her Jeep. She didn't seem to notice me, but I didn't even want to be near her. A few minutes later they both climbed into her Jeep and she revved her engine.

The Jeep turned and headed straight toward me. I had nowhere to go. The fear hit me like a sledgehammer. I didn't think she'd actually run over me, but at that moment I wasn't thinking. My eyes flicked to my car and to the treeline, both of them too far to run to. I took a deep breath and tried to keep walking, even as I heard the Jeep approach. She drove the car right across my path and skidded to a stop. The guy in the front seat was laughing, while Gretchen just sneered.

Randy. It was Randy from the hospital. I felt sick all over again. She really did know my secret, and now I knew why. I couldn't remember what his "issues" were, but it was definitely him.

Without saying anything, Gretchen tore out of the parking lot. I ran the rest of the way to my car, climbed in, and locked the door.

Gretchen would not only make life as difficult as possible, but she would tell people my biggest secret. A secret I hadn't intended to ever share with anybody. Mark would find out. What would he think of me?

But if I didn't come forward, I would live with this guilt that had attached itself to my heart—because I knew the right thing to do. And since I hadn't done anything yet and Gretchen was angry with me anyway, I didn't have any guarantees she wouldn't use the information against me even if I didn't say anything.

Trapped again. I screamed in frustration and then put my head down on the steering wheel. Eventually I started the car and went home.

Maybe I could convince my dad to transfer.

*   *   *

Even though the ride home was short, there was no doubt in my mind that I needed some help. Maybe not help, since I knew what advice my dad would give me, but maybe it was support I needed. To know that someone was in my corner, even if it felt like the rest of the world was in the other one.

But when I got home, Dad wasn't there. I fidgeted all through dinner and even offered to do the dishes for Lucy to burn off some nervous energy. She was pretty surprised. I fought with myself, wanting to change my mind and pretend nothing was happening, yet knowing I had to follow through. It was a good thing Dad showed up when the "tell your dad" side was winning. He knew instantly that something was bothering me.

"What's wrong?" he asked before he had even put down his briefcase.

I turned off the water and wiped my hands on a dish towel. "I guess I need to talk to you."

"Okay." He stood there with his briefcase.

"You can go ahead and eat and stuff. It's not urgent or anything." I obviously didn't convince him.

"Let's go in the family room and sit down."

I took a breath and followed him. Anna was on the floor watching TV, and Dad sent her upstairs and then settled into the recliner. I flopped on the couch and closed my eyes, searching for the words I needed.

I tried to think of the least shocking way to tell him. *Dad, the police are looking for me. No, definitely not. Dad, I know who started the fire last night. No, still too much.*

"Well, you know Gretchen, right? Well, I've been hanging around her a lot because of this play. Well, she kind of started this club . . . Well, I don't know what you would call it." I struggled to find the words as my dad sat patiently.

I took a deep breath. "Look, Dad, I was at the school when The Snack Shack burned down. I saw it happen. I wasn't in the building. I had nothing to do with the fire, but I know who did."

His eyebrows shot up. "You were there? Why . . . I mean, did you make the 911 call?" he asked.

I nodded.

"Well, you know we're going to have to go tell the police. You'll need to give them all the information you have."

"I know, but . . ."

"But what?

"It's just going to make things so . . . hard. Gretchen found out about me being in the hospital. She's threatening to tell everybody if I snitch on her."

"It might make things harder, but it doesn't really change the facts, does it?"

"No, I guess not." I was disappointed. I didn't know what I expected him to do differently, but he just wasn't very sympathetic about what this would do to my social life. It was more important to me than I realized. I had enjoyed being popular for a little while, and now it was all going to end. He didn't really understand.

"I'll go with you down to the police station. We should probably go now. We could end up being there for a while. Let me just get changed and we'll go."

I didn't move until he came back in. He had changed into jeans and was holding his car keys.

"You ready?"

"Yeah." I got up slowly, tossing the pillow I had been holding back onto the couch. "But maybe I can just tell them anonymously or something. They don't really have to know it was me, do they?"

"Beka." He sighed.

"I know. I know." I followed him out to the car and climbed in, knowing that once I told the police, everything was out of my hands. I hated carrying the secret, but I also hated destroying my life as I knew it.

But the more I thought about it, the more I realized I wasn't really enjoying the life I had been living. Sure, Gretchen made me more popular, but only if I stayed in her good graces. That wasn't an easy thing to do, and I had a feeling it was probably going to become impossible. I would have to choose between following God and following her. And I certainly didn't want to bow down to Gretchen. So, in effect, I knew I had to go and even knew it was for the best. But it didn't make me feel much better.

*　　*　　*

The police station was quiet, and the officer at the desk greeted us cheerfully, which struck me as strange, seeing as I was practically a criminal. Dad explained that we needed to talk to the detective in charge of the fire investigation, and the officer led us back to a small room with just a table and two chairs. We sat down and she dragged another chair in, screeching it across the floor before finally pushing it up underneath the table.

We waited a while before a tall African-American man in a suit walked in with a notepad. He immediately introduced himself, shaking my dad's hand.

"Mr. Madison., I'm Detective Sturgis. I understand you're here about the fire at the high school?"

"Yes, my daughter Rebekah has some information that she needs to share."

For the first time he turned his attention to me. He smiled warmly, but it didn't help my nerves. The whole time we had been waiting I had been trying to calm down my increasingly wild thoughts. I kept imagining the horrible things people would say about me for turning Gretchen in. And thinking about what Gretchen's version would be. And wondering if I'd be kicked out of school, thrown out of the play, or worse. Would it go on my permanent record? Could it keep me out of college?

"So, Rebekah, what can you tell me about this fire?" He smiled again, his pen poised above his notepad.

"Well, I . . . well." I was acutely aware of the fact that the words that came out of my mouth would profoundly affect my entire life. Did I really want to confess? It's not like I had too much of a choice at that point—but I still wondered if I could possibly get out of it. I looked at Dad for help.

"Go ahead," he urged.

Not much help.

"I was at the concession stand with a couple of other girls yesterday afternoon."

"How did you get in?" Detective Sturgis asked.

"One of the girls had a key."

"Who had the key?"

Now I would have to give up the name. I closed my eyes and took a deep breath. "Gretchen Stanley." He wrote the name down on his pad and looked up at me to continue. "We were all in there, and they had candles and stuff."

"What were you doing in there?"

It hadn't crossed my mind until that moment that I would have to be more specific about the witchcraft and my part in it all. I didn't really think the officer would care much about that detail, but my father? I didn't want to disappoint him yet again. And now I had no choice.

I looked between Detective Sturgis and my dad several times, trying to get up the courage to speak. I thought about asking if I could talk to the detective alone, but I didn't want to just hide it from my dad either. Secrets ate away at my soul, and I didn't want to carry this one any longer. I knew I would have to tell my dad sooner or later, and perhaps it would be easier to tell the story once and be done with it.

I took another deep breath.

"Gretchen has gotten into this New Age Wicca thing lately, and she wanted us all to make some vow and do some spell." I took a peek at my dad. His eyes were wide, but he didn't say anything. "I didn't want to do it, so I ended up arguing with Gretchen and then leaving. I went out by the team benches and sat there for a while. I was just getting ready to drive home when I saw the smoke and some flames. So I ran back to the Shack, but the door was locked. There was lots of smoke coming from under the door, but they didn't open it, so I ran and slammed up against it. That's when it finally opened. They all came out and went home. I ran back to the school and called 911."

"That's quite a story. So you weren't inside when the fire started?"

"No."

"Well, that information is very helpful. It's good you came forward. It was the right thing to do. Now what I need is for you to write down what you just told me. And you need to include the names of any other girls who were there."

"Am I in trouble?"

"Well, it would have been better if you had identified yourself from the beginning, but it sounds like you rescued those girls and notified the 911 dispatcher of the fire, so I'd say no, you aren't in trouble. But I'd be more careful who you spend time with."

I wrote out my statement, and then Dad and I went home. He didn't say anything to me at the police station or on the drive home, so by the time we got there my stomach was in a knot again.

"I'm sorry, Dad," I said once he stopped the car in the driveway.

He looked straight ahead out the window. I looked out my window to the right where the streetlights cast an eerie glow on the sidewalk and street. It was so quiet and still. I turned and looked back at my dad, who had now dropped his head and was staring at the keys in his hand. Finally he turned toward me.

"I don't know what to say, Beka. I'm proud of you for coming forward and for helping those girls, but . . . But you shouldn't have been there in the first place. What were you thinking?"

"I know. It was a mistake. I'm sorry."

"But why?"

"I don't know. Because if Gretchen likes you, school is a much more pleasant place to be. I didn't want to be on her hit list again. So I went along with it for a while. Until I just couldn't anymore."

"We'll have to talk again later. I need to sort through all this. And pray."

He climbed out of the car and went inside. I stayed in the car for a while, resting my head on the window.

And I still had to go to school in the morning.

In the morning, I saw Mai and Liz in the hallway at different times, so I relaxed, knowing that the police hadn't descended yet. But as soon as I got to homeroom, the intercom buzzed in our room and asked me to go to the principal's office.

This time I didn't have to wait. I was ushered straight into Mrs. Brynwit's office, where Detective Sturgis sat across from her desk. He smiled at me again, but I knew if he was at school, it would all go down that day.

"Rebekah, I understand that you were the 911 caller on Wednesday evening." Mrs. Brynwit's voice was sharp and angry.

"Yes, Ma'am."

"Well, Detective Sturgis is here to interview several other students about this incident. I would have appreciated you letting me know what was going on."

She was mad because I didn't tell her first? *I just can't win.*

"Detective, my secretary will call in the parents and show you a room where you can conduct your interviews." She led him out the doorway, and I stood to go as well. "Sit. I'm not finished yet."

I sat back down and watched as she spoke to her secretary. Then she came back in and sat down behind her desk.

"I received some information about those slanderous posts that have been going on our school bulletin board." She picked up a piece of paper that looked like it had been crumpled up and then smoothed out.

Even before she handed it to me, I knew what it was.

"Have you seen this?"

"Yes, Ma'am."

"Good answer. Because a student brought this to me just this morning and reported that they saw you throw this paper away a few days ago. Is this true?"

"Yes." *Who would go through the trash like that?*

"Then you admit that you lied to me about posting that story?"

"What? No, I didn't lie. It's not my paper."

"Miss Madison, I am getting very tired of your denials. This is a handwritten copy of the same story on the bulletin board, and you were seen with this paper."

"Yes, but it's not mine. Somebody gave that to me."

"If it wasn't you, then who was it?"

I suddenly realized that Mai was the one who had turned the paper in. And I realized that either I was going to get in trouble for it or I was going to have to turn Gretchen in.

"I'm sorry, Mrs. Brynwit, but I didn't do it. If you want to believe I did, then fine." I sat back in the chair. I was tired of turning people in, and I didn't need to make things worse.

"Then I have no choice but to suspend you. Effective immediately."

"But you can't. I didn't do anything." I could feel the tears coming.

"You either did it yourself or you're covering up for someone else. Either way I want you out of here now. We take slander very seriously around here. You'll have to come in with your parents for a meeting within twenty-four hours to formalize the suspension. But as of right now, you are to gather your things and go home."

I wanted to argue, but I was going to burst into tears any moment, so I just ran from the room. Halfway to the parking lot I realized I didn't even have my keys with me. I turned and headed back into the school, trying to wipe the tears from my face.

The bell rang as I reached my locker, but I kept my head down to hide my red eyes. I fumbled with the lock, and the tears started to slip down my cheeks again. I decided I would just wait there until everybody was back in class.

Then I heard Lori's cheerful voice next to me. "Hey. How did things go last night? I wanted to call you, but . . . What's wrong?"

I didn't move.

"Are you okay? Beka?" She pulled at my shoulder until I turned and looked at her.

"What happened?"

I couldn't stop crying. Thankfully the halls had begun to clear out. "Suspended" was all I could choke out. "The play, everything, gone. I got suspended."

"But you didn't have anything to do with the fire."

"Not that. The post about you. They think I did it."

"But you said it was Gretchen," she said carefully.

"It was! I swear it was."

"Then why are you getting suspended?"

"I couldn't turn her in. Lori, I just turned her into the police last night. I'm tired of being a rat."

She didn't say anything for a few moments. I wiped at my face some more, trying to compose myself.

Lori took a deep breath. "Fine, then I'll be the rat." Lori hurried off down the hallway. I took off after her.

"Lori, what are you going to do?"

"Don't worry, Beka. I'll take care of this."

I didn't say anything else. Lori pushed open the door to the office and told the secretary she had to see Mrs. Brynwit immediately. The secretary got on her phone, and a few minutes later she gestured toward the principal's office.

"Mrs. Brynwit? I'm Lori Trent."

I hovered in the doorway. Mrs. Brynwit glared at me. "What are you doing here? You were told to go home."

"There's been a mistake," Lori said quickly. "I wanted to let you know that Beka did not write that story about me. It was Gretchen Stanley." Lori looked over at me.

I swallowed the lump in my throat.

"Gretchen can't stand me and was just trying to hurt me. I didn't want Beka to get in trouble for something Gretchen did."

"Sit down, both of you," Mrs. Brynwit ordered. I sat but didn't say another word. Lori explained about the posts, how she had seen the notebook paper herself, and that she could vouch for me that I didn't post them. It took a while, but Mrs. Brynwit finally relented and reinstated me, though she still looked angry as a hornet when she sent us back to class.

"Thank you, Lori."

"No problem. Gretchen hates me anyway."

"Well, she hates me now too."

I filled Lori in on the details of my visit to the station last night. When I finished she threw her arms around me and gave me a hug.

"I'm so glad you did it. Don't you feel better?"

"Not really."

"Well, you will eventually. When it's not all still such a mess."

I wasn't so sure, but I went back to class and tried to focus on the rest of the day.

*   *   *

By the time I got to seventh period, all sorts of people knew that at least Gretchen and Mai were involved in The Snack Shack fire. I tried to keep a low profile, but nobody connected me to it. Yet. I knew it was only a matter of time. Jen Burk, our student editor, was all over the story, assigning a whole team of people to get the scoop so that we could publish it in the next issue of *The Bragg About.*

Ms. Adams came and sat down at the table I was working at. "Beka?" Her voice was a whisper. "I know what happened last night. I think what you did was very brave. It shows integrity, and you made sure the truth was known. I'd like you to be our student editor next year. If you're willing."

I smiled for the first time in days. "Really?"

"Really. And I'd like you to write the feature on the fire. When we get the go-ahead from the administration."

"Oh, I don't know. Maybe Jen should handle it. I mean . . ."

"I think you're the one who should do it. I think you will handle the story with care and integrity."

I nodded weakly. The bell rang and I made my way to rehearsal. I could tell word was getting out, because on the way to my locker two different conversations were halted when I walked by. I also got some "looks" from a couple of kids. I sighed. It didn't surprise me, but it wasn't any fun. I wondered how long I would be the pariah.

*   *   *

I sat onstage with the rest of the cast once I changed into my costume. With only a week left to opening night, we were doing rehearsals in full dress. Thompson came out onstage, and just as we were all about to stand for the voice warm-ups, he made us all sit back down.

He cleared his throat. "Gretchen Stanley, Mai Tanigawa, and Liz Ortlund will no longer be a part of this cast." There was a collective gasp from the entire stage. "I will assign two people to play the parts of Pepper and Sophie and, of course, Beka Madison will be Annie."

Everyone turned and looked at me. It took a full minute before the reality of what Thompson had just said sank in. I was going to have to be Annie.

*   *   *

"You don't want to be Annie?" Julie asked when I sat in her office that afternoon.

"Not really. I know the part, I think, but all those people? What if I freeze?" I didn't really want to talk about the play, since it made me more nervous and fluttery inside just to think about it.

"Your opening night is next week?" she asked.

I nodded. She smiled and started to say something, then frowned and flipped open the folder that she held underneath her notepad. "That's the night you lost your mother." She spoke with a sadness to her voice as if she felt my loss. We both sat there looking at each other, me remembering and she waiting with me in the moment.

"I lost my mother too. When I was eighteen. I was at college for my freshman year, having fun and taking classes, and then I got a phone call one night." She didn't go on, but she didn't have to. I knew that horror. That devastation that pounces on you and then proceeds to tear apart everything underneath you until you're not sure you can stand one moment longer.

We talked for a while about my mom. Julie just let me talk about the things I remembered. The things I missed. I didn't tell her what scared me the most—her not being around for all the important moments still to come in my life. I figured that was a discussion for another day.

But that was when going to counseling didn't seem all that bad anymore. I even had a brief moment about being sorry that I would have to miss next week's appointment. Especially when she stood with me at the door when it was time for me to leave.

"I'd like to come see you in the play next weekend. Would you be okay with that?"

"Sure. I just hope there's a play to see."

"Don't worry another moment about it. You'll do just fine. I believe in you."

The gesture warmed the spots inside that were scared and frantic. Even if she had never seen me onstage and really didn't have any way of knowing if I would do okay, it didn't matter. The words made a difference anyway. It was only a play. I could make it through a play, couldn't I?

The next week was positively a blur. Thompson kept us late at rehearsals almost every night, and I barely had time to eat and do my homework. Gretchen had been suspended from school, so I hadn't seen her since the Thursday after the fire. I was so grateful that I didn't have to run into her, because I had enough pressure without adding that. Liz and Mai were in school but were not allowed to participate in the play. Apparently, since Gretchen provided access to the Shack, she was being held responsible. Mai just glared at me whenever she saw me, but Liz actually came up to me that Wednesday.

"Beka? Can we talk for a minute?"

She had found me at my locker. One look and I knew she wasn't mad at me, so I closed my locker and leaned against it. "Sure. What's up?"

"I just wanted to thank you."

"Thank me? Well, I wasn't expecting that."

"Yeah, well, if you hadn't told the police, I would have had to. There was no way I could deal with that kind of secret."

"Me neither."

"So, I'm glad you had the guts to do it. I wish I had had the guts to leave when you did. I just didn't feel right about all that stuff Gretchen was doing. But we've always been friends. I've just always done what she did."

"Well, that's what I was doing too until I realized that I just couldn't anymore. I didn't like what she was doing. I was tired of being a droid."

Liz laughed and tossed her ponytail off her shoulder. "I guess that just about describes me." She paused for a minute. "You know, I go to church too."

"Oh?" I wasn't sure what else to say. *Good for you?* Or maybe she was trying to ask me about God. "I went to church for years before I understood what it really meant."

She gave me a small, relieved smile. "Well, I better be going. Maybe we can talk later?"

"Sure." I smiled. She walked toward the cafeteria, and I left in the other direction. I was surprised and pleased. It was nice to get support from an unexpected place.

*   *   *

I was doing fine with the lines, the blocking, and the songs for *Annie*, but my big problem was having to do it in front of an audience. I still had no idea what that was going to be like, and I wasn't sure what effect it would have on my memory, or my stomach for that matter. Not only that, but Paul had announced the play during Sunday school, so Nancy, Allison, Morgan, and Rachel were all going to come opening night. Even worse was that Josh was coming too. He had come up to me after class and said that he couldn't wait to see me. I had just smiled dumbly, since I was too flustered to speak. He seemed to have that effect on me.

Thompson had pronounced me ready at Thursday's rehearsal, so he sent us all home with orders to get plenty of rest and to be at school by six o'clock to get ready for the eight o'clock curtain. I drove home with very mixed feelings. On the one hand, I was probably as prepared as I could be, but I still had to actually do it. I was going to have to walk out onstage, in front of people I knew, and sing and dance and act. Once more I had gotten in over my head. My only hope was that God would help me remember what I was supposed to do up there and keep the contents of my stomach inside instead of outside.

*   *   *

At home, everybody else was so excited that I felt out of sorts. Even Lucy was dying to see the play and mentioned repeatedly that she'd finally get the chance to be in a musical when she came to high school next year. I kind of wished I could give her my part now.

Dad pulled me aside after dinner and asked me to go for a walk with him. We hadn't walked together since before Mom died. It was his way of talking to us about something, so I knew it wasn't just to enjoy the early spring evening. It was cool enough for sweatshirts, so I slipped one on and went out to the driveway where he was waiting for me.

"Hey, Butterfly. You ready?"

I nodded and we turned left out of the driveway. We walked for several minutes before he said anything.

"I've been thinking about what happened last week," he started. "And I need to apologize to you."

"Me? I'm the one that messed up. Again."

"Yes, you made a mistake. And I need to remember that you will make mistakes sometimes. I was angry about it, and I'm sorry for that. Will you forgive me?"

"Sure, but I still don't see why you should be sorry. I just keep messing things up."

"Beka, you realized your mistake and dealt with it. A little later than I would have liked, but you did deal with it. It shows you're maturing."

I didn't respond, because I felt like I was pretty immature a majority of the time. It was almost embarrassing that I let Gretchen lead me around by the nose. She was the reason I was even in the play. Everything led back to her.

"And there's another thing. I feel like I failed you as a father because you struggled through it all by yourself. It took a building burning down for me to find out what was going on. I got angry because, in a way, I thought that if your mom had been around she would have known. She would have been able to help earlier."

"But, Dad, I'm the one who doesn't let anyone help me. It's just hard for me to admit it when I'm in a bind because it's usually my own fault for being there."

"Will you work on that?" He smiled. "Because I'm here for you."

"I know. And I'll try. At least this time I didn't end up in the hospital." As soon as the words left my mouth, my heart dropped to the street. Gretchen was going to tell. She was probably using her suspension to plot her revenge.

"What's wrong?"

"It's just that Gretchen still knows about the hospital. She's going to tell everybody."

"And?"

"And I don't know. There's nothing I can do about it."

"Maybe not, but remember that God is on your side too. Ask Him to help you through it."

I didn't say anything, but it would have been nicer if God rescued me out of it instead of just helping me get through it. Or maybe He could get Gretchen's family to move to Michigan. Not that Michigan deserved that.

*   *   *

I was the first one to show up at the school. I even beat Thompson there, because the rear door was still locked. I sat against the brick wall in the alcove and waited, trying not to make myself more nervous.

"You ready?" Thompson asked when he came around the corner and saw me sitting there.

I smiled a little. "Sort of."

He opened the door and propped it with a brick. "You'll be fine."

Great or *wonderful* would have been a more encouraging adjective, but I would settle for fine as long as I didn't do anything embarrassing like forget what I was supposed to do. I went to my little tiny dressing room. They were letting us use the practice rooms for the play and all the leads had one. It felt weird being in there, because I still thought of it as Gretchen's dressing room. I touched the fabric of the red and white dress I wore during the second part of the play and the wig they had thought they wouldn't have to use.

I started the tedious task of pinning up all my long hair so that it would stay hidden beneath the wig. It was a pain, but I wasn't about to cut my hair. I had gotten half of it up when there was a knock at the door. I turned in my chair to see Mark leaning in the open doorway. He grinned and I puddled, just a little.

"So you ready for tonight?"

"Thompson asked me the same thing, but do I really have a choice? Whether I'm ready or not, that curtain is still going to go up." I turned back to my hair, gathering a long strand, twisting it up with my finger, and then pinning it.

He came in and closed the door slightly.

I kept pinning my hair.

"So I talked to my parents."

"Yeah, so." My voice may have sounded blasé, but inside I perked up.

"So they're reconsidering."

"And that means what?"

"Well, it means they might let me date again. And you know what that means."

"Why don't you spell it out for me?"

"What's wrong? I thought you'd be happy," he said.

I glanced in the mirror at his reflection. He looked annoyed.

I turned around in my chair. "Mark, shouldn't we have this conversation after your parents have decided? I mean, you're not sure, right?"

"Right. But I do know I can go to the junior prom."

"Oh." That shut me up. I didn't have to look in the mirror to know I looked ridiculous, and now I could feel my face turning red. Lovely.

He took my hand and held it for a moment and then said, "Rebekah, would you go to the junior prom with me?"

I didn't know what I should do about my feelings for him, but it was my feelings for him that made it impossible to say no. "Yes" was all I could choke out.

"Great!" He jumped to his feet. "Break a leg tonight. You'll do fabulous." He leaned down and kissed me on the cheek, and then he was gone. It was several minutes before I gained my composure and could return to my hair. The butterflies in my stomach were now dancing with the butterflies in my heart.

*   *   *

Once I had my wig, makeup, and orphan costume on, we did voice warm-ups in the band room. My throat had felt tight and dry, but the warm-ups helped to relax me just a little bit. When we finished I paced in the band room, but I could only do tight little circles. I was leaving to go find a hallway when I ran into Liz. She seemed sad.

"Hi. I'm sorry you're missing all this," I said.

"Well, it's my own fault. Maybe next year. Have you heard what happened?"

"No, what?"

"They didn't charge any of us with arson or anything like that since it really was an accident, but we did get charged with trespassing."

"Oh no."

"No, it could have been a lot worse. We all got probation and we have to do community service and stuff. Oh, and Mrs. Brynwit decided that we have to help with every fund-raiser the boosters have over the summer and next year. It really could have been worse."

"So, are you going to watch the play?"

"Yeah, I can't just miss it. Even though someone else has my part."

"I think I'd like to miss it." I smiled weakly.

"Once you get out there you'll do fine. It's normal to be nervous. Even Gretchen would have been nervous, and she thinks she was born for the stage."

"Well, I better go pace before it starts." We said good-bye, and I used the hallway to the left of the stage to walk back and forth. It helped get rid of some of the nervous energy.

I was on my third lap when I saw Josh standing near the dressing rooms talking to Michael Goodall. He turned just at that moment and caught my eye. He said something to Michael and headed toward me.

He had roses in his hand.

And I was suddenly aware of my grubby orphan look and the curly red wig on top of my head.

"Hey there. I wanted to give you these." He held out the bouquet of roses, and even though it seemed so typical, I buried my nose in the red petals and inhaled. I had never gotten roses from a guy before.

"Thank you." I smiled at him but was at a loss for what else to say.

"I've been looking forward to this all week. Can I pray for you?"

I nodded but was a bit awestruck. Another first for me. He put his hand on my shoulder and bowed his head. "Father, I come to ask You that You help Beka to know Your peace tonight. That she would remember everything she needs to and rests in the palm of Your hand."

I took a deep breath and looked up as he lifted his eyes to mine. We stood there to the point of me feeling awkward.

"Thank you." *Can't you think of anything else to say?*

"Well, I better go find my seat. We'll talk afterward, okay?"

I nodded. *Mute, again.*

*   *   *

Those of us in the first scene went out on the stage a bit before the curtain and got our bearings. Everybody seemed to have the jitters, but I was the one who was Annie. If I blew it, the play would be over. I took a deep breath and tried to regain that peace I had felt when Josh was praying. It wouldn't do me any good to think of every disaster that could happen.

A couple of the other orphans were peeking through the curtain at the audience. We could hear them through the curtain, talking, coughing, and getting themselves situated. I went to the curtain to wait for a turn to peek. I thought maybe I shouldn't look, but my curiosity got the best of me. I would just look to see where my family was sitting and maybe Josh.

I pulled back the heavy red curtain just enough to see through with one eye. There were so many people that I swallowed hard. It looked like there wouldn't be an empty seat once everybody sat down. I was still scanning the crowd for my family when I saw her.

Gretchen was sitting in the front row. Dead center.

I nervously looked away, even though I knew she couldn't see me. I still wanted to know where my dad was, so I kept looking, trying to put Gretchen out of my thoughts. I found them in the center section, over to the right. Lucy was looking at the program with Anna, and Dad was playing with our video camera. I breathed a sigh of relief when I saw that Gabby wasn't with them. I hadn't said anything directly, but I had been dropping hints. I was glad Dad had picked up on it.

One surprise was that Paul was talking to Josh. Josh sitting with my family was an odd sight. Even though I knew he was friends with Paul, they had never been really close until lately. I wondered if that was because of me. Then I saw Nancy in the row right behind them, along with Allison and Morgan. I was about to move away to give someone else a turn when I took one more look at Gretchen. Her hair was blonde again, and her arms were folded across her chest. She was practically scowling, as if she was willing us all to trip and break our noses.

I turned away from the curtain and went to my spot. I had to sing the very first song of the play after a few lines with Rachel, who was now playing the role of Molly. I closed my eyes and tried to think of what it would be like to really be Annie.

Michael Goodall streaked across the stage, whispering, "Two minutes, two minutes."

I heard the audience applauding as the band came in and took their seats, and then the curtains were pulled back, revealing blackness with dozens of tiny red lights. I grinned. For some reason, all these people holding little video cameras struck me as funny.

Then I felt the lights come up.

And I disappeared.

*   *   *

When the curtain closed the entire cast let out a deafening war whoop. I think the entire cast came and gave me a hug and told me how great I was. All I knew is that I had gotten through the entire play without missing a line or a note. I did manage to be in the wrong spot during one of the dances, but nobody but the other orphans would have known.

I had never been so relieved. I knew that I had five more performances to get through, but the first one was done. The others would be easier. I went back to my dressing room still basking in all the praise. Thompson came up to me and told me I had done a "fabulous job" and that I had to promise to try out next year. I didn't promise. Even though it was fun to have an audience, to hear them respond, I still didn't want to have to do it again. It was too stressful.

Lots of people streamed backstage from the audience. I looked around, knowing my dad would come back soon. They all appeared a few minutes later, Josh in tow.

"Wow, Beka. I had no idea you had it in you," Paul said, giving me a hug.

"You were the best singer. Some people sang really bad," Anna added. Lucy covered her mouth.

"It was really great, Beka. You sang beautifully," my dad said, handing me a bouquet of wildflowers.

I thanked them all, still feeling a little embarrassed from all the attention, and told them I had to go change. They fell in with the crowd, waving good-bye. I turned to head back to my dressing room, tired and happy, when someone caught my arm.

I turned and was face-to-face, or face to chest really, with Josh.

"Oh, hi," I said.

"Hi. That was incredible. I didn't know you could sing like that!"

I blushed. "I guess everybody knows now." At least it was different from thank you.

"Well, I better let you get changed. I'll see you Sunday." He waved and also disappeared into the crowd.

I finally got to my dressing room, where Lori was waiting with another bouquet of flowers.

"That was amazing, Beka, really."

"You really think so? I mean, everybody is being awfully nice, but . . ."

"No, really. I'm sure you were much better than Gretchen would have been."

"I don't know. This is great and everything, but I'll be glad when my life gets back to normal."

I thought about that for a second. With Mark and Josh and Gretchen all in my life, maybe it would never be normal again.

"Well," she said, "Mom and Dad—" she grinned— "are waiting for me, so I'm going to go. But I'll be back tomorrow night."

"Really?"

"Yep. I'm going to come every night to make sure Gretchen doesn't try to throw anything at you."

"Thanks a lot. One more thing to worry about." I laughed.

"No worries," she said. "I've got your back." She gave me a hug and said good-bye.

*   *   *

I finally settled down in front of the mirror and took off my makeup and the wig, removing all traces of Annie, leaving behind just me, freckles and all. I hung up my costume so it would be ready for tomorrow. A lot of the cast was already gone when I came out. I knew that there were several parties that night, but I didn't feel like going to a party. I felt like being alone. I wasn't sad; I just was so overwhelmed that I wanted some time to settle my thoughts. I shut off the lights and closed the door. I had done well, and the feeling gave me this sense of satisfaction. Mom would have been proud of me.

The rest of the performances went very well, though none of them were quite as magical as that first night. Lori was at every performance, true to her word, and Josh came once more, bringing more flowers. Gretchen had come back to school and was completely ignoring me, though she couldn't have been very happy about all the attention I was getting. I knew she'd drop the bomb eventually, but I assumed she would wait until she wasn't in so much trouble. Liz told me that Mrs. Brynwit was keeping close tabs on her.

So maybe I would have some time before I had to deal with her again. In the meantime I had two formal dances coming up. Two dates with two guys. I couldn't believe that I went from never being noticed at all to having the attention of two guys. Mark had already wormed his way into my heart, but Josh was making some major dents as well.

*   *   *

I chose a flower from every one of the bouquets I got and took them to my mother's grave one morning after the play was over. The chill was out of the air, and the trees were all beginning to bud. The pollen made my nose itch, so I sat there sneezing and crying, telling my mom how much I missed her. I didn't know if she could hear me. I thought that God might pass on the message to her if she couldn't. I wished that she was around to help me pick out dresses and help me put up my hair with braids and tiny flowers.

And it was only the beginning of my life without her.

I tried not to let my mind wander to the dances and graduations she would miss. To my wedding that I hoped I would have one day. Who would I call when I grew up and had my own babies? I didn't try to stop the tears. I just let them fall, knowing that keeping them inside almost hurt more.

I took a deep breath of the fresh air and tried to remember that even though she was gone, I wasn't alone. God had come through for me more than once, and even though I was still going to have to face the consequences of standing up to Gretchen, there was a part of me that felt stronger for it.

Once I stopped crying my thoughts turned to Mark

and Josh. Nothing in my life could ever be simple. Mark had captured my attention first with his charm and good looks, but Josh was never far from my thoughts lately. There was something safe about him that I didn't feel with Mark. And now I had an official date with both of them. A prom and a formal. I would have to get a dress, maybe two. I tried to imagine how my mom would do my hair if she were still there. How she would talk and laugh with me, give me advice, and then let me go.

Letting go.

That was exactly what I had to try to do. Let go of all the what-ifs and could-have-beens. I didn't want to move on without her, but in my heart I knew she wouldn't want me to wallow in my sorrow either. I still had God. I took another deep breath. Maybe He would find a way to fill in the gaps for me.

It was just a shame that God couldn't braid my hair.

Visit
www.becomingbeka.com

You'll find:

- ❑ small group discussion question for *The Masquerade* and *The Alliance*—"God-Powered Girls"
- ❑ more information about Beka and the author
- ❑ contests and other cool stuff
- ❑ a way to sign up for a free e-mail newsletter
- ❑ a place to Raise Your Voice!

Thanks for reading!

Sarah

ISBN: 0-8024-6451-3

Beka has been trying to move on with her life since her mother's tragic accident, but it feels like she's going nowhere fast.

Things are not so good at home. Beka's brother and sisters won't leave her alone. Her scary dreams keep coming back. Her dad's new female friend starts showing up. And worst of all, Beka has a secret she can't share with anyone, especially not her family. Her big secret is turning into lots of smaller secrets, and she's not sure how much longer she can hold everything together.

As it turns out, Beka's not the only person with secrets. But before she can get a new start on life, she'll have to be honest about who she is.

Will Beka face up to the truth before something drastic happens?

MOODY
PUBLISHERS

THE NAME YOU CAN TRUST.

1-800-678-6928 www.MoodyPublishers.org

Since 1894, Moody Publishers has been dedicated to equip and motivate people to advance the cause of Christ by publishing evangelical Christian literature and other media for all ages, around the world. Because we are a ministry of the Moody Bible Institute of Chicago, a portion of the proceeds from the sale of this book go to train the next generation of Christian leaders.

If we may serve you in any way in your spiritual journey toward understanding Christ and the Christian life, please contact us at www.moodypublishers.com.

"All Scripture is God-breathed and is useful for teaching, rebuking, correcting and training in righteousness, so that the man of God may be thoroughly equipped for every good work."
—2 TIMOTHY 3:16, 17

MOODY
PUBLISHERS

THE NAME YOU CAN TRUST®

THE ALLIANCE TEAM

ACQUIRING EDITOR
Michele Straubel

COPY EDITOR
Cheryl Dunlop

BACK COVER COPY
Julie-Allyson Ieron

COVER DESIGN
Barb Fisher, LeVan Fisher Design

INTERIOR DESIGN
Ragont Design

PRINTING AND BINDING
Dickinson Press Inc.

The typeface for the text of this book is
Aetna JY